From Falling ~~on~~ for the Billionaire

Large, warm hands righted her. Vicky sat for a moment on oaken male thighs, simply getting her breath back. Palms burned through the yellow dress, branding her ribs.

Good heavens. She was in Sinclair's lap. His legs were under hers, his muscled torso pressed against her side. Her mouth was level with his...her body burned. Mortified, she wiggled to get off him.

His hands tightened. The dress was slippery, and her wriggling slid his hand smack into the undercurve of her breast.

A breast that suddenly was stiff and full. She squeaked. "I...I'm sorry."

"Don't apologize," he growled. His eyes were very dark indeed, pupils fully dilated. She could see the brush of individual hairs in his eyebrows, the long, thick lashes...

The curtain opened again. "Well? What are you waiting for—?"

Vicky swiveled to see Ronnie's face morph from annoyed to stunned.

Purest Delight! "...fun, exciting and a little naughty..." —Guilty Pleasures Book Reviews on *Edie and the CEO*

Recommended Read! "*Edie and the CEO* by **Mary Hughes** is a pure delight. The dialogue is fresh, fun, and witty, the suspense is just enough to pique your curiosity, and the love is so endearing that it will make your heart sing...This is one magnificent story that you don't want to miss. Bravo Ms. Hughes! You've hit a home run with *Edie and the CEO* and I'll definitely be recommending it to my friends." —Blackraven's Reviews on *Edie and the CEO*

Can tripping over your own feet lead to falling...in love?

Media superstar Zan Sinclair runs with a rich, exclusive set, thanks to his hit communications show, *Revealing Secrets*. But he's tired of high-gloss, meaningless dates. He just wants to meet a nice girl—like shy Dr. Vicky Brooks, sister of his international model ex-girlfriend, Ronnie.

He texts Ronnie to arrange a casual meeting at the CommuniCon convention in Kansas City. Problem is, Ronnie gets the wrong idea. She thinks Zan wants to get back together with her.

When Vicky's twin wants help winning back an ex-boyfriend, kindhearted Vicky can't say no. But Ronnie's ex is Vicky's longtime crush, smart, sexy Dr. Alexander Sinclair. Now the safe-from-afar crush is shockingly real, making her heart pound, making her want...more.

How can Vicky and Zan finally meet...and more...without sending Ronnie into a jealous rage? Worse, will Zan's posh friends ever accept shy Vicky?

Look for these titles by Mary Hughes

Now Available:

Romantic Adventure
Edie and the CEO—Crimson Romance
Falling ~~on~~ for the Billionaire
Cin Wikkid: April Fools For Love
Hot Chips and Sand
Bad Boy Billionaire's Lady: Lovless Brothers
Playing With Fire: The Battle of the Bands

Biting Love/The Ancients
Bite My Fire—Entangled
Biting Nixie—Entangled
The Bite of Silence—Entangled
Biting Me Softly—Entangled
Biting Oz—Entangled
Beauty Bites—Entangled
Downbeat—Entangled
Assassins Bite—Entangled
Passion Bites—Entangled

Biting Love Nibbles
Night's Caress—Entangled

Pull of the Moon Series
Prophecy Mates
Heart Mates
Hunt Mates
Mind Mates

Standalone
Black Diamond Jinn

Coming Soon:

The Classic Billionaire's Newshound (Lovless Brothers)
The Genius Billionaire's Hacker (Lovless Brothers)
Night's Kiss (The Ancients)
Night's Bliss (The Ancients)
Soul Mates (Pull of the Moon)

Falling ~~on~~ for the Billionaire

A Romantic Comedy

Mary Hughes

DEDICATION

To my husband Gregg, for laughing at my jokes.

To author friends Leigh Morgan, Edie Ramer, Elle J. Rossi, and Roxy Mews. You make writing a lot less lonely. Love you guys!

To you, dear reader, for joining me in this story.

Thanks to Blue Otter Editing and EJR Digital Art for adding polish and panache.

CHAPTER ONE

Vicky Brooks was at her kitchen table, peacefully grading papers, when international model Ronnie Rivers phoned to drop the bombshell on her.

"This weekend, sister dearest," Ronnie said. "CommuniCon. I'm going—and so are you."

"I am?" *Uh-oh.* Vicky laid her pen carefully atop the papers. She was a successful junior college teacher, but somehow her twin's schemes always managed to land her in trouble, starting when they were seven and Ronnie's "looking beautiful" ended up with Vicky caked in their mother's expensive lipstick and eye shadow when the spanks got handed out.

Vicky loved her sister and knew Ronnie's plans weren't malicious. She was just overly efficient about getting other people to meet her needs.

"CommuniCon. The communications convention in Kansas City?" Vicky stifled her stampede reflex in order to hear her twin out. Besides, she was already registered—where could she stampede to? "I just saw you last week when I visited you in Los Angeles. Much as I'd love to see you again, why do you want me to go?"

"Because *I'm* going, silly," Ronnie said brightly. "We'll be seen by the beautiful people and shop for hours and have such fun!"

1

"Says the woman who flosses her behind in the name of fashion. Can you make 'fun' sound any less like 'root canal'?"

"They're called thongs, Vicky, and they give the glutes definition while avoiding embarrassing panty lines. What's wrong with being seen?"

"Nothing, except you know what happens when I'm seen. I'll photo-bomb without even trying."

"It's not your fault you're not photogenic."

And that was why Vicky put up with all her sister's machinations. Ronnie always defended her in her own way.

"Besides, that's my job," Ronnie continued breezily. "Looking good."

"Looking great, Ms. Supermodel. Your job to be seen, my job to think."

"You can think while we're shopping. C'mon, Vicky, it's not healthy for you to stay home reading all the time."

"Reading is perfectly normal. *I'm* perfectly normal." Sometimes Vicky wished she didn't have to defend herself.

"Of course you are," Ronnie said quickly. "I'm sorry. I just want to see you happy. I love you."

"I love you too." Vicky smiled and shook her head. "Let's talk about something else. How is your acting going?"

"I'm working my way up," Ronnie enthused. "I've got a role in *Crime Scenes: LA*. A dead body, but Dead Body #1, which means I have two scenes, one where I get discovered and one where the stars have a big discussion over me. Lots of screen time."

"Soon you'll be getting lines yourself." Vicky tucked the phone under her chin, picked up her pen, and started correcting the next paper.

"That's why I'm going to CommuniCon, for the classes on emotional presentation. They'll help my acting."

Vicky paused in her grading. She'd learned to listen to what *wasn't* said as much as to what was. "And...?"

"No other reason."

"Veronica Lynn Brooks. You're lying so badly, if Mom catches you, you won't sit down for a week."

There was an embarrassed pause. "Damn. How do you do that?"

"That's *my* profession."

"Well, if you must know...Alex will be there. I think he wants to get back together."

Vicky flinched, dropping her pen. "Dr. Sinclair?"

Alexander Sinclair, PhD and billionaire rock star communications expert, had shot straight to international fame and fortune while still gathering professional kudos. Dating him, being seen in his Lambo, had thrust Ronnie's career into overdrive. They'd since broken up—amicably—as he only dated anyone a couple months.

Vicky knew Sinclair would be at the convention. She'd heard he'd signed up last minute. Here might be the reason why. "Ronnie. You *think* Zan Sinclair wants to date you again, or he *told* you?"

"His friends call him Alex."

Vicky shook her head impatiently. Of all the things for her to pick up on...though her sister was wrong. Ronnie might have dated him, but Vicky knew more about Dr. Alexander Sinclair, far too much. Sinclair's friends called him Zan, not Alex. "You're avoiding the question. Did Sinclair tell you or not?"

"He texted me about the acting classes at CommuniCon. And he's going. What else could that mean? Vicky, please. You have to help me land him again."

"*I* do? Why?" More importantly, *how?* Vicky was a middle-class academic, while Sinclair was a billionaire genius. She tended to get a touch tongue-tied around handsome men. And rich men. And brilliant men. Sinclair was all three.

Worse, she'd crushed on him for years—from afar, all safe and secure that she'd never actually have to talk to him.

Now Ronnie wanted her to cruise directly into his path? Meeting him for real, Vicky would trip over her lolling tongue, bad enough. With her sister's schemes, how many ways could that go *really* wrong?

She took a deep breath, trying to calm herself, but it didn't work. She bleated, "Ronnie, I *can't.*"

"You *have* to. He's the best boyfriend I ever had. Please? Pretty please?"

Vicky's heart pounded harder. She was fighting a losing battle. "Why him? Because he's rich and handsome?"

"*All* the men I date are rich and handsome," Ronnie retorted. "But Alex is smart. So smart, he could practically read my mind."

"Yeah." Being a nonverbal communications genius would do that. She speared a hand through her hair. Helping her sister land this particular big fish was the last thing she wanted to do. But they were sisters—Veronica and Victoria Brooks forever. Although her sister had shed her twin name for Ronnie Rivers, short and snappy, great for a sound bite or a head shot.

Didn't change the fact that her twin needed her.

Still, she tried one last time. "Ronnie, that convention was sold out months ago. You can't register—"

"I pulled some strings. I managed two spots, although it was hard to pay for you, since I'm a bit short on funds right now. The acting is costing more than I expected, and the time eats into my modeling..."

Vicky clenched her eyes against the inevitable. "Get your money back. I'm already registered."

"*Awe*-some. I'll see you Thursday." In the endearing singsong she'd perfected in childhood, Ronnie rang off with "Love you! Buh-bye."

* * *

Thursday at the convention, Vicky wandered the hotel, searching for the best place to wait for her sister. CommuniCon packed a whirlwind of sessions into four days, and events, vendors, and goodies were crammed into every nook and cranny of the hotel. She finally decided the conference registration area, in the atrium off the lobby, was the best place to meet up with friends.

She stationed herself beside a marble-clad pillar near the tables and people-watched for half an hour before she heard, "Yoo-hoo, Vicky! Darling, here I am."

Her sister waved enthusiastically in the big arch between lobby and atrium. Ronnie's blonde hair was covered with a silk scarf, and her eyes were shielded with big smoky glasses in best vintage Hollywood style.

Smiling in return, Vicky started toward the registration tables, but Ronnie headed straight for a little coffee cart parked near a pillar on the opposite side of the room. Vicky closed her eyes briefly; she'd already cruised by and noted the prices. She loved coffee but didn't love paying ten dollars a cup. Dutifully, she pushed through the crowd to join her sister, hoping Ronnie didn't expect her to buy, but knowing her sister probably hadn't thought that far ahead.

Sometimes being the smart, sensible one sucked.

"This convention is bigger than I thought it would be." Ronnie whipped off her glasses, revealing eyes as green as emeralds—she'd apparently taken to wearing contacts as well as dying her brown hair blonde. "For it not being in Los Angeles."

Vicky suppressed a smile. Ronnie's idea of geography was Google shopping. "Kansas City isn't one of the big three, but it's a central hub for the United States. It's a real city, Ronnie."

"So I see." She waved at someone. "Otherwise the Dragons wouldn't be here."

Vicky followed her gaze. Two women sat just inside a fashionable storefront cafe. One was slender and smart in a tweed skirt set, her short, shining silver bob the only clue to her age. She returned Ronnie's wave. The other, with aggressively styled red hair, masses of chunky jewelry, and an ensemble that screamed trendy, pointedly ignored them.

"Who are the Dragons?" Vicky asked.

"Style mavens. Gatekeepers for the Right Set, or at least the set Alex belongs to. Leda Loper is the Greater Dragon. She's the one who waved. She's a huge stickler for good manners and good taste."

Ronnie held up two fingers to the coffee vendor. "Two skinny mocha lattes. The Lesser Dragon is Lolly Darling. We call her Lady LaLa, though not to her face. Oopsies, forgot my cash." With a sweet smile at the vendor, she waved Vicky forward.

Vicky sighed and pulled out her wallet. "They're in communications?"

"No, of course not. They're probably here because of Alex. Speaking of...you're going to be my wingman, right?"

Joy and rapture. A front row seat to watch Ronnie land Zan Sinclair was a special circle of hell. Vicky wanted to sob in frustration, despite not having a snowball's chance with sizzling-hot bachelor Sinclair herself. She was shy and liked to read. He was the biggest name in communications. She lectured to half-empty rooms of bored freshmen. He'd catapulted to fame when his show *Revealing Secrets* was the sleeper hit of the year, and he entertained millions. He was rich, a billionaire at least. She wouldn't even know a Prada if it bit her.

"Vicky? My wingman, right?" Ronnie prodded her with a long, lacquered nail.

"I would, but..." She paid and put her wallet away. Sinclair was handsome and articulate, and she could almost see the disaster. He'd smile and say a simple "Hi," and she'd stutter and melt into a puddle of goo. "Are you sure you weren't misreading his text? What about his three-date limit?"

When it was over between them the first time, Vicky felt bad for Ronnie. But she'd also felt rather sorry for Sinclair. All those supermodels, starlets, and rich daughters—how had he not found a single person to share his life with?

"Maybe it's just three consecutive dates." Ronnie shrugged elegant shoulders. "Or maybe I'm the exception."

"Ladies?" The coffee vendor held out two cardboard-wrapped, capped cups. "Your lattes."

Ronnie snagged hers. "Come on. I want to see the goodies room."

Vicky barely snared her own cup before Ronnie latched on to her elbow and dragged her away. The last thing Vicky saw of the registration table was three people hanging a ten-foot poster of Dr. Sinclair. She sighed. He was so handsome, his dark eyes gleaming with intelligence. Just seeing his picture made her want to swoon like a Victorian heroine.

She sighed. She'd been crushing on him too long. Mega-rich media star versus poorly paid junior college lecturer? They were from different worlds.

But Ronnie was from his world. If she could make him happy, if he made her happy, who was Vicky to stop them? In fact, wasn't it her job to do everything she could to facilitate them? However personally painful it was?

She sighed and accepted the inevitable. "Wingman."

"Great!" Ronnie happily dragged Vicky into the vendor display room, also known as the goodies room. "I'm hoping he'll introduce me to his producer."

"Who?"

"Alex's producer is a real name in the business." Ronnie stopped at a booth filled with high-resolution webcams.

Vicky picked up a brochure. The tool helped students read expressions and identify emotions. She touched a webcam. Her finger sprang up, two feet tall, on a flat-panel monitor. She jerked back. "Why do you want to meet a producer?" Stuffing the brochure into her convention bag, she picked up the software's accompanying manual and flipped through it.

Ronnie pulled Vicky tight, so fast Vicky dropped the manual. She whispered in Vicky's ear, "I'm nearly thirty. I know that doesn't mean much to you, but modeling's a young woman's game. And it's *cutthroat*. I won't last forever."

"But...but you're sought after worldwide. You're at the peak of your career."

"The peak, yeah. You know what that means." Ronnie bent over the webcam. Her left nostril filled the whole screen, along with the barest shadow of a wrinkle. "No direction to go but down."

Vicky blinked, suddenly understanding. "That's why you're trying to break into television."

"Which means meeting Alex's producer. Which means getting back in Alex's good graces."

This was about more than Ronnie's love life. It weighed on her whole future.

"All right, sister," Vicky said. "I'll not only be your wingman—I'll be the best darned wingman you've ever had."

* * *

Alexander Sinclair slid from the presenters' greenroom near the CommuniCon registration desk, twitching straight the sleeves of his Kiton K50 suit while he scanned the masses of people in the atrium. He searched for two particular heads, one silver-blonde and one plain brown. As he was taller than most of the people here, he quickly saw the pair he sought weren't in the room.

Zan wasn't disappointed. Half of doing any job well was not letting extraneous emotions get in the way. It was ninety-nine percent of doing *his* job well. Effective communications relied on clear channels, free of clogging feelings. He had a plan, and he executed it efficiently. Moving into the hallway he made his way to the next room.

The pair wasn't in that room either, but he simply proceeded to the next, and the next. His careful planning and patience was rewarded when, in the swag room, he saw the toned blonde.

At first he didn't see the blonde's sister and nearly panicked. But no, Veronica, in her platform heels, was simply half a head taller than her twin. There. The slender brunette stood nearby, reading a manual.

Dr. Victoria Brooks.

A zing of pleasure shot through him, quickly suppressed but not ignored. Though he didn't indulge in his emotions, he did have them. He especially had them around *her.*

Strange to feel so strongly about a person he'd never actually met.

But if things went the way he hoped they might, he'd remedy that soon enough. Ronnie would introduce them. She might even think it was her idea.

"Dr. Sinclair?"

Nearby, a woman waved at him. He didn't know her, but she knew him. That happened a lot these days, a part of the fame gig. He smiled as she rushed up, offering an open convention booklet and pen. He signed his name, chatting easily with her while she stood with a slightly dazed smile. Finishing with a flourish, he pressed her booklet and pen into her hands, nodded goodbye, and strode toward the sisters.

They were close in conversation, looking as different as fraternal twins possibly could. He hadn't a clue they were sisters when he'd first seen Dr. Brooks in a series of homemade teaching videos on the Internet. He'd immediately been struck by her. She looked smart, sweet, and genuine. In her most recent video, posted three weeks ago, she'd invited students to connect with her at CommuniCon. Lonely, he'd planned on trying to meet her here.

The conference organizer, Josiah Johnson, had been most helpful when Zan called to arrange a late berth. Almost too helpful—he'd wanted to ax the keynote speaker for Zan. Zan had explained that he'd rather attend for pleasure—and had gotten assigned as a speaker anyway.

He'd discovered only after it was too late that Vicky Brooks was related to one of his ex-girlfriends.

He remembered Ronnie Rivers. Fun, a touch self-centered—not that unusual for models—and easy to please.

But also easy to anger.

The problem was, if this didn't happen in exactly the right way, Ronnie might get jealous. Not a problem if she only got angry with him. But she might lash out against Vicky. So he'd pretend to be surprised when Ronnie introduced him to her sister. He'd ask if the two of them were hungry—a few minutes after noon, it was highly probable. He'd take them both to lunch. Talk with both of them equally. Make plans for dinner, with both. Take them shopping; Ronnie liked shopping.

He wondered briefly if Vicky liked shopping, too. Soon, now, he'd find out. Another thrill of excitement rushed through him at the thought.

With his height and build, he cut easily through the crowd. Now that he was out from between the pillars, several people recognized him—well, nearly everybody did, but most only smiled or nodded. He smiled back but kept cleaving through. A few people tried to stop him for his autograph, but he had slips on hand for just this purpose—head-of-the-line passes for his autograph sessions during the convention. He kept his focus on the sisters and kept moving.

About halfway across the room, Ronnie saw him. She waved, just as the crowd thickened with people clamoring for autograph slips, and blocked his view.

He tamped down his frustration and slid from the grasping fingers.

Then a tug on his back suit coat flap—a tug *down*—turned him.

A child of maybe eight stood there, eyes hopeful, autograph book extended.

Touched, he stopped to sign her open book and handed it back with a smile, touched even more when she whooped and trotted happily away with it.

His attention had been off the sisters for only a few moments, but when he resumed plowing through the last of the crowd to where they'd been, only Ronnie's silver-blonde head was there.

"Alex, darling. So good to see you." She offered her cheek.

He gave her the expected double air buss, using the mimed pecks to search for Vicky. He couldn't quite believe that she was gone.

"Who are you looking for?" A faint double line appeared between the model's big green eyes, the only sign she allowed herself of a frown. A blatant warning to a man like him.

He straightened. As casually as possible, he said, "I thought I saw you with someone."

Ronnie's eyes narrowed.

Red alert. He recognized that expression. Not jealousy, but its prickly precursor. *Think fast, Sinclair.* His brain worked like lightning. "I only mention it because...my friend Nate Winters was talking about getting some lunch. I saw the two of you and thought we could make it a foursome."

"Oh." Ronnie slid her manicured hands over his. "Are you hungry? I'm starving. My sister is off listening to some boring presentation. Let's ditch your friend Winters and go somewhere nice."

CHAPTER TWO

Zan sat at a window table twenty stories up with a lovely view of the city, enjoying an appetizer of a very good salmon with cream and shallots, an excellent Czech Pilsner, and Ronnie's conversation. Well, Ronnie's monologue. He'd originally been a college professor, so put a quarter in him and he'd spout exactly fifty minutes of lecture. But at least he had a stop button.

She was happily chattering away about her cover shoots, her dress for the convention's big dance, and her latest foray into acting as Body #1, whatever that was, encouraged only by his occasional nod or *umm-hmm.*

On the plus side, it left him free to think.

He spent the appetizers wondering what had gone wrong. Missing his expected introduction to Vicky, he felt off-kilter. He poked gingerly at his emotions and was shocked to realize he'd been looking forward to meeting her with an eagerness that bordered on impatience—very uncharacteristic of him.

Normally it wasn't so hard for him to meet a woman. But this wasn't any woman. This was Ronnie's sister; Ronnie herself was the complication. If he hadn't dated Ronnie...but he had, needing a new date for something or other. The damned three-date limit, which, thanks to his friend Nate, ensured a succession of meaningless relations. Ronnie wasn't the best or the worst or even the most memorable.

"I have to say, Alex, I was surprised to get your text."

That jolted him out of his thoughts. He focused on Ronnie. She was looking at him expectantly. "Why is that?"

"Well, your three-date rule and all. Why do you have that silly rule, anyway?"

He sat straighter. It was as if she'd read his thoughts from his face. He had to remember that Ronnie, for all her batting eyelashes and toothy smiles, was the sister of a smart communications professional and really quite shrewd.

"It's because of a friend," he admitted. "He got himself into a sticky situation with a star-struck heiress. Though he only dated her for a couple months, somehow she decided it meant marriage." Nate still owed Zan for extracting him from that, though not before a lot of unhappiness, regrets, and bitterness spilled on both sides.

"So we've had three dates," Ronnie said. "An art show, an awards program, and...did we have a third date?"

"The symphony." Going through that experience with Nate, Zan had instituted the three-date rule, so he never endured or created that kind of bitterness. He also always made damned sure he gave each woman plenty while they were seeing each other and also at the end, to ensure no woman parted with him in anger. With Ronnie, he'd not only given her the usual expensive gifts, he'd helped her land a lucrative modeling contract with an international cosmetics company.

"And when you gave me a lift from the airport a couple weeks ago? Wasn't that a fourth date?"

"No. That was doing you a favor." Which was the second time he'd seen Dr. Brooks and realized there was a complication named Ronnie Rivers.

Ronnie had called him, saying something about dropping off her visiting sister's rental car. He wondered about that—Ronnie could afford a limo back from the airport. Although fortunes often changed in LA, and maybe she was conserving. He liked to maintain friendly relations with his ex-dates, so he rearranged his calendar and obliged her.

That day was burned into his brain. He drove to the airport—he liked driving, and despite employing a chauffeur, often took the wheel himself—his mind on work. There were some show details to nail down and some facts to double-check before signing off on the current script. He made a mental note to have his post-docs do that. He drove competently along I-405 while his brain chewed on the various items.

Arriving at LAX, he saw Ronnie Rivers's silver-blonde head, pulled into the pickup lane, and slowed.

Only as he neared did he realize Ronnie was talking with a petite brunette whose back was to him. The brunette wore her hair with the top pulled back in a clip, the rest flowing past her shoulders in that pretty yet practical style he'd always liked. He dated supermodels but, in fact, was more attracted to the girl next door. Not too many of those in his circles though. Besides, they were often intimidated by his money.

The nice-looking brunette hugged Ronnie. Real affection, which frankly surprised him in a town known for its polite air kisses.

The brunette's slim fingers wrapped around the handle of her suitcase, and she turned to go inside.

He saw her profile.

His heart jumped. He jammed on the brakes automatically.

She had the loveliest nose, a little long, a touch sharp, but he liked the forthrightness it implied. Like Ronnie's, only Ronnie reduced hers with makeup to beauty while the brunette's nose had personality.

Her cheekbone was softly stunning, her jawline firm and perfect. A delicate eyebrow feathered over a long fringe of lashes. The crescent of a heavenly blue iris beckoned.

He sat there, stunned. Hooked. She looked bright, pretty, and, well, nice.

He'd always dated supermodels. He'd never dated a nice girl. He wanted to now, with a ferocity that shocked him.

Then she was gone, inside the terminal.

And he realized two things. First, that was the woman he'd seen on the teaching videos. She was petite and even sweeter-looking in person.

Second, meeting her at the convention was going to be more complicated than he'd thought.

"Damn it," he muttered.

"What did you say?"

He looked up to see Ronnie's eyes on him, sparking green with suspicion. He realized his fork was hovering in midair, and it had been for some time. "Oh. Nothing. I just bit a peppercorn." He carefully chewed and swallowed, then gave her his most captivating smile.

"I see."

He was afraid she did see, too clearly. Which wouldn't have been a problem, but he'd learned she was the jealous sort that day when, pulling away from the curb at the airport, he'd asked her about the brunette. "Who was she?"

"Who was *who*?" Both Ronnie's brows had risen.

Here be dangerous waters. He'd shrugged. "I saw you with a woman and wondered."

"It's nobody," Ronnie had said shortly. "Just my sister Vicky. Thank you for picking me up.

My sister. Picking *me* up.

He'd wanted to meet Vicky, but he knew he had to defuse that streak of jealousy before he did. What if Ronnie took it badly? That was no way to start a long-term relationship.

16

He'd been rather surprised at that thought. Had he decided, from a few streaming videos and a single in-person look, he wanted a lasting relationship with Vicky Brooks?

But no, he was simply ensuring that *if* he and Vicky had a future, it would start cleanly.

Of course he was.

So in order to meet Vicky in a way that wouldn't get her sister sore, he had to get Ronnie to introduce them.

At which point he'd had a brainstorm. What did the three of them have in common? Communications. He and Vicky were communication scientists, and Ronnie wanted to break into acting. If Ronnie came to CommuniCon, she'd get some training in expressing emotions, and he could enter into the sisters' sphere casually.

Getting Nate Winters onboard to teach his famous acting seminar had been a hurdle—his best friend knew there was something up. but Zan wanted everything natural and didn't want to give Nate any details.

Conference organizer Josiah Johnson had again been almost too helpful when Zan had called to get Winters included, asking if Dr. Sinclair wanted the keynote speaker axed in favor of Dr. Winters? Poor keynote speaker.

Still, it was little enough hassle to meet the woman who'd been constantly on his mind since he'd seen her videos, then that heavenly sliver of blue iris.

To pique Ronnie's interest, he'd texted her, casually mentioning he'd be at the convention, that Nate was doing a thing on acting, and was she going? Ronnie had texted back immediately that of course she was.

But then, at the moment of truth, Vicky had disappeared. *Why? Where had she gone?* He fisted his hand...corralled his emotions and breathed deeply instead, pressing it out to a five count. *Calm.* Feelings would only cloud his judgment.

So what did he do now? Try again tomorrow?

No. The con ended Sunday. Waste a whole day? Tomorrow was too late.

"Are you going to the Gala, Alex?" Ronnie asked brightly.

He nodded. Ronnie started talking about Gala this and Gala that. He forked up his entree, a rather nice medallion of beef. The Gala was Saturday night, a black-tie and long-dress affair if he remembered correctly. Ronnie's shape lent itself particularly well to long, sleek skirts, probably why she was so excited.

Vicky's slim backside would look good in a long skirt too. Which distracted him rather pleasantly for a moment.

"You'd be perfect," Ronnie was saying. "Those boring pre-dinner drinks and then sitting through that long lavish dinner...I'd love to have someone interesting to talk to." She set her elbows on the table, perched her chin on her joined hands, and smiled brightly at him.

A finely honed sense of self-preservation dragged him up from his absorption with Vicky to pay full attention to the blonde. Implications sparkled in her unnaturally green eyes.

Well, hell. Ronnie was dancing around the idea that he, Zan, should escort her to the Gala. "Aren't you sitting with your sister?"

"Well...I don't have to. I mean, she's here for work. She probably has tons of boring professorly socializing to do."

"It's my profession too," he pointed out dryly.

She rolled her eyes. "But you don't act like it. You're interesting." Then she pursed her lips thoughtfully, overdoing it. Zan could see she'd gotten impatient with coy hints and was about to come right out and ask.

He wedged words in first. "I'd ask you but..." Desperately he tried to think up a way to get out of this with his skin whole. "I'm at the head table with all the other boring lecturers."

She clapped her hands. "Wonderful! I'd love to sit front and center."

"*Boring*, Ronnie." He was totally screwed. Ronnie adored garnering attention. She'd worm her way in unless he could avoid it in the next ten seconds. "Communications wonks, the other presenters, and Nate Winters, and..." Salvation hit in the form of an idea. "And you could *both* sit with *us*."

A quizzical smile raised the corner of her glossy, full lips. "Both, who?"

"You and your sister. You can *both* sit with Nate and me."

"Oh. Hmm." Her tiny little forehead line sprang into being, her version of a frown; she was about to reject the idea. He braced himself. Sure enough, she said, "Vicky's Gala dress isn't fashionable. And she's shy. Well, she calls it introverted, but it's the same thing, isn't it? She won't want to sit at the head table."

"Too bad." He shrugged, pretending not to care, but he could feel his jaw tighten. He stabbed a piece of beef and shoved it into his mouth to cover his tension. Chewed and swallowed. "Nate and I are both dateless for the Gala." It was a risk, admitting that— it as good as ensured that she'd slot herself in. But he was desperate. "Two lovely women on our arms...it would have to be two, to keep the numbers even. But if you don't think your sister would want to sit in front—"

"She might, if I ask her."

Yes.

"But..."

Aw, no.

"You really wouldn't want her up there."

"I wouldn't?"

She made a noise. "Not with the dress she has."

"Ah." And then he had an idea, a good idea, so good he almost felt he was as brilliant as everyone told him he was. "But *you* could take her shopping and help her find a fashionable one, couldn't you?"

"Well, sure. But I'm a bit cash poor now..."

"Of course." He pulled out his wallet and offered his credit card. "You could get yourself something, too."

Ronnie snatched the plastic. "I'll convince her."

He hid his smile of relief. "That's settled then." As casually as he could, he added, "You should introduce us beforehand."

Ronnie's slight frown returned. "You want to meet Vicky? She's just a professor, you know. Not even a full professor. She's at a community college, for heaven's sake."

"But she's your sister, Ronnie." He kept the frustration from his voice, giving her a brilliant smile. "Shouldn't I meet your sister?"

Her frown deepened a moment as her brain worked, chewing at his words. Then the line disappeared, replaced by a smile even more blinding than his. "Of course, Alex. I'd love for you to meet a member of my family."

Zan's smile froze. *Meet the family.*

This was how Nate had almost gotten himself married.

CHAPTER THREE

"And?" Vicky sat across from her sister at a front table in the trendy Butterbuns Coffee Shop, sipping herbal tea with lots of honey. Honey added calories, always a concern with her petite frame—a little went a long way—but crowds made her nervous, and she needed both the heat and the sweetness. She wondered again why she'd decided to come to the convention. She enjoyed the sessions, which generated amazing ideas for her, and she liked the people, but this many packed together gave her a headache.

Oh yes. The possibility that one of the three hundred views her teaching videos had received included a poor student who wanted her help.

"*And* what?" Ronnie stirred her sugar-free latte, a coy smile playing over her lips.

"How was your big reunion?"

"Wonderful!" All Ronnie's pretense dropped. "We had a lovely, intimate, *expensive* lunch and talked for ages."

Vicky found herself smiling. She loved her sister's ability to throw herself joyously, wholeheartedly, into something.

"Guess what? He wants me to go to the Gala with him!"

"Oh." Vicky's smile faded. She'd have to sit alone. Still, Ronnie was happy. Vicky pasted on a sickly smile. "Lovely for you."

"Isn't it?" Ronnie's smile turned calculating. "He wants *you* to go too."

"Me?" An arrow of shocked pleasure pierced Vicky. Sinclair wanted her? "Why? He doesn't even know me."

"No, but he knows *me*, and he wants *me* at the head table with him. But for *me* to sit there, he has to find someone for Nate Winters. That's you."

"Dr. Nathaniel Winters?" Vicky's pleasant tummy fluttering turned distinctly agitated. Winters was second only to Sinclair in popularity and wealth. He was a friend of Sinclair's, often appearing on his show.

Ronnie giggled. "It's like a double date, see?"

"A double...?" Vicky trailed off as the horror hit her. "I'm supposed to be Dr. Winters's *date to the Gala*?"

"What, is he an ogre or something?" Ronnie's nose wrinkled, the closest she got to screwing up her face in distaste. "Ugly?"

"No, not at all." Dark-haired, blue-eyed, and athletic, Nate Winters was often on eligible bachelors lists, though usually a few ranks down from Sinclair.

And she, Dr. Vicky Brooks, introvert extraordinaire and simple community college teacher, was supposed to sit at dinner and make scintillating conversation with someone as brilliant as Winters? She started hyperventilating. "I...I can't. I don't have a thing to wear."

"Yes, I know."

Vicky's breathing eased. "So you *know* I can't—"

"Alex gave me his credit card. It's another sign he wants me back." Ronnie's smile was smug.

"Nice." Vicky's breathing slowed, and her heart rate eased. Ronnie was no longer talking about setting her up with Dr. Winters. Vicky was very glad her sister was off that scary topic of dating a gorgeous, out-of-her-league man...

Then Ronnie's words seeped through. "Wait. Dr. Sinclair gave you his credit card? Why? What are you buying yourself?"

"Silly goose. We're buying *you* a dress, for the Gala. We're going shopping!"

✳ ✳ ✳

Vicky skittered in her sister's wake through the intimidating glass-and-gold door of Chez Michal's Haute Couture. She followed as tightly as she could decently get without fusing to Ronnie's backside.

From the outside, the hotel boutique screamed exclusive money. Vicky was almost disappointed the inside wasn't wallpapered in Franklins. A trio of well-dressed women shopping there, as Vicky stumbled through on Ronnie's heels, turned their beautifully coiffed heads and gave Vicky the exact same *you're hopeless* smirk. Her stomach plummeted to her ankles.

Baring her unfashionable body to a room full of judgmental women? It promised to be as painful as the time Ronnie had accidentally set Vicky's hair on fire with the curling iron. She wanted to poke out her eyes with a fish fork.

On the plus side, when Ronnie flashed Sinclair's mega-ultra card, the head salesperson whisked them off to a private room. On the negative, the room was wall-to-wall mirrors. Next to Ronnie's glorious golden curls, Vicky couldn't help seeing how plain her clipped brown hair was.

"Only the best for the Gala." The salesperson was a slim woman with hair slicked back into a twist, her nametag reading "Monique." She toted in an armload of gowns, bustling them to Vicky for approval.

None of the gorgeous gowns had a price tag, rocketing Vicky's stomach from her feet into her throat. "But Ronnie, what if we spend too much? Won't Dr. Sinclair get mad?"

"Alex doesn't get mad. Not about a little thing like money. That buttercup dress on top is nice."

"We shouldn't take advantage of his kindness." Yet Vicky couldn't help reaching toward the gorgeous confection on top. She fingered its silky, sheer overdress. *This is what luxury feels like.*

"Oh, pooh," Ronnie said. "That's why he gave me the card. Besides, I saw the cutest pair of heels that will go perfectly with my Gala dress." She turned to the salesperson. "Get that pair of Montrousseaux heels, the ones in ruby and diamond crystals and gold satin."

"Yes, Mademoiselle Rivers." The salesperson hung the dresses on a rack and started out.

"Wait," Ronnie said, and when the salesperson stopped, she added, "Bring the matching scarf and purse too."

"Yes, Mademoiselle." Monique took a step.

"Wait. You might as well add the crystal and ruby earrings. Those will contrast nicely with the gold lamé."

The salesperson arched one thin brow. "Does Mademoiselle also want the matching crystal and ruby necklace?"

Vicky winced at the not-so-subtle acid in the woman's voice.

"Good idea," Ronnie said. "Well, what are you standing there for? Go!"

"Mademoiselle." The salesperson briskly departed.

Ronnie turned on Vicky. "What are *you* waiting for? Off with those...I guess you call them clothes. C'mon, peel down to your underwear."

Yikes. "My underwear? Do you want a repeat of third grade gym class?"

"You're still wearing pink-flowered long johns?" Ronnie pinched the bridge of her nose. "We'll buy you real lingerie. Strip."

"Not long johns. But this is a conference, for heaven's sake. I'm not supposed to be half-naked in a dress boutique. I'm *supposed* to be sucking in lectures and presentations, absorbing knowledge like a sponge—"

"Victoria Emma Brooks." Ronnie's eyes flared. "You're going to absorb my palm applied sharply to your behind if you don't do as I say." She pointed one long red fingernail. "*Strip.*"

Vicky stripped.

"Oh for cripes sake." Ronnie's moue became actual disapproval.

Vicky looked down at herself. Not flowered long johns, but Saint Lucas take her, she was wearing her Star Wars underwear, complete with Wookie bandoleer cross-the-heart bra. At her sister's rolled eyes, she wanted to become one with the floor.

Naturally, that was when the salesperson returned. Monique stopped so fast her heels made a tire-squealing noise. At least, that was what it sounded like to Vicky's hot ears.

"Well." Slowly Monique set down the pile of red-and-white crystal-spangled gold. "Mademoiselle will need underwear."

Vicky's whole face fired. "That's Dr. Mademoiselle," she muttered. It only made her feel a little better.

When Monique disappeared again, Ronnie leafed through the gowns. "This one, I think." She tugged a pink confection from the packed rack.

"Um, pink isn't exactly my color."

"Don't be silly. Pink is everyone's color."

As her blonde sister carried the dress toward her, it did reflect Ronnie's cream-colored complexion in a flattering way.

Vicky put it on hopefully. As Ronnie zipped up the back, she dared a peek in the mirror.

A cotton-candy machine had eaten her.

The salesperson returned with satin-covered hangers dangling wisps of ivory and white. Again she stopped short, heels screeching just as judgmentally, eyes as big as saucers.

Ronnie beamed. "Isn't it lovely?"

"Lovely." Monique's lips compressed. "But perhaps the pink would not, er, complement your gold gown, Mademoiselle Rivers?"

Vicky closed her eyes in silent thanks. People with eyes the world over would thank the woman.

"I hadn't thought of that," Ronnie said. "Maybe a nice powder blue?"

Vicky opened her eyes in time to see Ronnie hold up a dress like wadded gas-station windshield wipes on a hanger. Vicky slapped a hand over her face.

"Mademoiselle Rivers," Monique said. "Perhaps you would check the fit of the Montrousseaux items while I assist your sister?"

"Good idea." Ronnie dropped the hanger and picked up the shawl, admiring it against her cheek. The crystals tinkled softly as she moved.

The moment Ronnie was distracted, instead of forcing the awful wadded gown on Vicky, the salesperson considered her, tapping the soft end of a satin hanger against her chin.

A moment later, her expression cleared. "The forest green."

She swept Vicky onto a platform in the center of a set of mirrors. Vicky was confronted with an infinite ring of herself in the pink barf. She closed her eyes before she had an epileptic seizure. She wasn't prone to them but had heard they were linked to trauma. The pink thing certainly qualified.

"Let's get Mademoiselle into something a bit sleeker, shall we?"

A rasp of zipper and the weight of tulle fell from her. Soft clouds were thrust into her hand. She opened her eyes. Six Vickys held scraps of silk and soft lace much sexier than her Wookie bandoleer.

"The foundations must bring honor to the gown," the salesperson said. "Well? Put them on."

"Um, okay." Vicky started to slide the tiny bikinis over her briefs.

"What are you...*no!*" Monique glared. "Do not defile the lovely Siren Wisps set with those...those..." She pointed at Vicky's undies, finger trembling. "Those."

"Right. I just thought there'd be panty shields—"

"Strip!"

"Stripping." Vicky got off the pedestal first. No way she was baring her naked flesh to all those mirrors. She'd get a mirror rash or something.

Monique rooted through the rack of dresses. "Aha!" She slid out a long sheath. Deep green at first, it shimmered from sapphire to emerald as the light hit it different ways. She turned with the gown. Her gaze landed on where Vicky hid behind one of the mirrors, and she *tsked.* "The foundation garments, *please.*"

Vicky smiled weakly. "You got it."

The salesperson hung the gown on a hook near the mirrors. "Change while I get Mademoiselle Rivers's jewelry." She glared at Vicky then swept out.

Vicky wasn't a communications specialist for nothing. That glare promised severe butt paddling should she dawdle. She peeled off the Wookie bandoleer.

Ronnie came over and fingered the green sheath gown. "I don't know about this. I've never seen you as a winter."

"Well, if I'm going with Winters... Get it?" But when Vicky slipped on the ivory bra, all puns dropped from her head.

Her breasts were cupped in clouds. *Nice.* She could get used to expensive undies if they all felt like this.

She reminded herself that Dr. Sinclair was paying for it. *Zan Sinclair is buying the silk sliding against my naked breasts.* She shivered at the thought.

Ronnie lifted the gown from the hook and held it against herself. "It is pretty." She considered herself in the mirrors. "Narrow, though. You'd have to be quite slender to carry it off properly. Oh well, you'll be sitting mostly."

Vicky exchanged her panties for silky triangles joined by cute bows at the hips. She looked down at herself.

And sucked in her gut.

The salesperson returned, bearing an exquisite set of red and white gemstone jewelry. Ronnie immediately dropped the gown to hustle over. "Exactly what my dress needs." She grabbed the boxes from the salesperson like a kid seizing Halloween candy.

The woman was left with a single slim package. She brought it to Vicky. "Hose for Mademoiselle."

Vicky crinkled her nose. Pantyhose came in three varieties: baggy, scratchy, and boa constrictor. She normally wore slacks or jeans, dressing in skirt suits on only three occasions—winter graduation, spring graduation, and the annual Departmental Meet & Greet for faculty and staff.

But Monique was glaring death-paddles again. Vicky smiled, sat in a nearby satin-cushioned chair, and slid the hose on.

She pulled on air. She stood and drew the fine material over her thighs and hips. Like smoothing the silkiest cream over her legs. Wonder of wonders, the top fit with a whisper of control, smoothing the line of her hips perfectly.

Vicky stared at herself in the mirror. Slowly, she became aware her jaw hung loose, creaking slightly in the breeze. Not really, but it felt that way. She closed it with a snap.

"There." The salesperson beamed. "Now the gown." She picked up the pooled sheath from where Ronnie had dropped it, slid it off its hanger, and indicated with a flick of manicured nails that Vicky should raise her arms. When Vicky did, the woman dropped the gown over her head.

It slithered down Vicky's body with the same silky feel as the hose. Form-fitting over bosom, waist, and hips, a long slit showed off lengths of calf and thigh.

With her petite figure, she expected the sheath dress to make her look like a green pencil, or worse, a green stuffed sausage.

Instead, she looked like a woman with a lovely figure.

Monique guided Vicky up onto the pedestal. Her eyes rose to the mirrors.

She froze.

The green made her washed-denim eyes into big brilliant sapphires. Her too-pale skin was now pure ivory with a delicate blue undertone, pink at the cheeks and carnation at the lips. Her teeth were sparkling white.

The dress made everything pop.

"I'm...I'm..."

"Mademoiselle is beautiful," the salesperson breathed.

Ronnie looked up from where she was trying on the crystal and ruby earrings. Her eyes met Vicky's in the mirror and widened. "You look gorgeous, Vicky." Her voice was as soft as the salesperson's.

But it wasn't filled with reverence. "In fact, you look better than me."

CHAPTER FOUR

Vicky immediately dropped off the pedestal. "Of course I don't," she said to her sister. "On Dr. Sinclair's arm, you'll be the most beautiful woman in the room by far. I'm just your wingman."

Ronnie stood stiffly a moment longer then relaxed as she let herself be mollified. "True."

Vicky heaved a silent sigh. Her sister wasn't intentionally difficult, but when she was unhappy, it bled off her, making everyone around her miserable too.

But when Ronnie was happy, she was just as infectious.

Vicky had been turning the tide of Ronnie's emotions since childhood and knew just what to do. She followed flattery with distraction. "Why don't you tell me about those shoes?"

"Oh, aren't they cute? Real Austrian crystal, and the color will offset my dress perfectly..."

As Ronnie chatted, Vicky cast a glance out of the corner of her eye at herself. Hard to believe that was her in the mirror. The green sheath not only looked gorgeous...in it, she felt feminine and, for the first time, beautiful. As if, even in a roomful of gorgeous women, Sinclair might notice her, just a little bit.

She lost her breath at the thought.

Then she shook her head. Took a cleansing breath, in and out. Sinclair was Ronnie's. Even if he found Vicky...attractive, what a thought...she had to

30

give her sister a clear field. True, Ronnie had never done the same—she'd unintentionally swept away every boy interested in Vicky—but that wasn't Ronnie's fault. Boys and Ronnie were like iron filings to a magnet. Couldn't blame the magnet for being irresistible, right?

But for a heartbeat, as Vicky gazed sideways into a mirror, she wished Sinclair would see her in the green dress and maybe think she was, not only pretty, but as pretty as her sister.

Ah, she was being ridiculous. Like he'd see what no other man had. She turned resolutely away. She was no beauty, no international model, to interest such a rich, sophisticated man. That was a fantasy, like all the times she'd watched him on television and dreamed.

Well, that was what she was good at, wasn't it? An introvert, a person of the mind. Great imagination. But underneath...

She yanked the dress down and peeled the fancy bra away to reveal the true geek underneath.

An ordinary woman, despite the crown of mirrors.

Realistically, about the best she could hope for was that Sinclair found her interesting. Stimulating. A worthy colleague.

Also ridiculous, really. After all, he was an internationally known and respected star. She was an untenured professor at a junior college.

In the mirror, her shoulders slumped, the dress pooling around her ankles and the bra hanging from her hand. Oh, who was she kidding? She wasn't anywhere near Sinclair, not in looks or smarts or money or accomplishments. Even Ronnie wasn't a match, but as a supermodel, she was closer than Vicky.

Vicky straightened. She was here to help her sister get back together with him. Then at least two of the three of them would be happy.

* * *

Vicky and her twin left the boutique at three, Monique promising the green gown's alterations would be done in time for Vicky's final fitting Saturday at ten. *Just two days from now I'll be sitting at dinner with Nate Winters, a few chairs down from Zan Sinclair.* It seemed incredible.

The sisters went back to the conference to check out the ballroom and locate the venues for Ronnie's acting seminars.

Vicky threaded through the packed crowd in Ronnie's wake, thinking about the gorgeous green dress, *not* fantasizing about Dr. Sinclair's brilliant dark eyes widening as she glided into the room— okay, maybe a little—when a young woman staffing a table outside the ballroom waved at her. "Dr. Brooks! Yoo-hoo, Dr. Brooks."

Vicky cleared her head to squint at the woman. She recognized one of her students at her St. Louis community college. "Janette? What are you doing here?"

"My mom is on the convention committee. She hooked me into helping out."

"Lucky you." Vicky tapped Ronnie on the shoulder. Ronnie glanced back with a raised brow. Vicky waved *come with me* then cut her way through the mass of people crowded around where Janette sat in front of a pair of doors.

"Hey," a woman snarled. "No line skippers." She was a tall, leathery woman with an incongruous tattoo of a kitten on her forearm.

Vicky raised both brows. This mob was a *line*?

A glance at the electronic event board outside the doors showed why the crowd had formed—Nathaniel Winters was speaking at four o'clock. It was only three fifteen. Winters was that popular. "I'm not skipping," Vicky said. I'm just talking to Janette."

"You'd better be." With a final scowl, the leathery woman turned frontward.

Vicky nudged through until she stood before a banquet-style table draped with floor-sweeping white linen where Janette sat. "You have to ride herd on the mob trying to snag seats for Dr. Winters? You must really love your mom."

"It's not so bad." Janette grinned. "It's ticket only. I don't have to lasso anyone. I just have to take tickets."

"Ah." Vicky tried to see the end of the line, but it was mob all the way down. "Hey, Ronnie." She turned to her sister. "This is one of your acting sessions. Maybe you should get in line. You do have a ticket, right?"

"Sure. But standing in line? Please. That's for peasants."

"Hey," the leathery woman yelped. "No line jumping."

The woman wasn't snarling at Vicky this time, or even her sister. No, cutting past everyone was a woman with aggressively styled red hair and chunky jewelry—and an upraised middle finger. Lolly Darling, Vicky remembered. Her sister had called her the Lesser Dragon, one of the style mavens of Zan Sinclair's set.

Lolly headed straight for the doors.

"Ma'am, wait." Janette jumped to her feet as Lolly breezed past and tugged open one of the ballroom doors. Janette slapped the door shut. "Ma'am, you can't go in yet. They're not ready."

"Young woman." Lolly drew herself straight and looked down her very long nose at the unfortunate Janette. "Do you know who I am?"

"No, ma'am. But unless you're Dr. Nathaniel Winters, you can't go in. And frankly, you don't have the rugged jawline or the powerful chest."

Way to go, Janette.

"How *dare* you. I'm Lolly Darling, Leda Loper's bosom companion and one of Nate Winters's very best personal friends. Let me in at once!" She gave Janette's arm a vicious pinch. Janette yelped.

"Hey." Vicky moved to intervene. She was shy, but her inner lion came out when someone else was in trouble.

Ronnie snared her arm and whispered, "Don't. Lolly can be cruel, and she has no conscience. And she can really hold a grudge."

"I have to." But as Vicky prepared to act, she saw Janette had recovered.

The young woman blocked the doorway with her body. Janette's eyes were narrowed at Lolly. "Personal friend? I bet you don't even have a ticket."

"You little worm. I'll have you stricken from this convention. From the hotel! Now let me pass." Lolly yanked open the door despite Janette, nearly knocking the poor young woman off her feet.

As Vicky surged forward, Ronnie said, "You'll regret it later."

"Then I'll regret it." Vicky seized Lolly's arm before she could swing into the ballroom. "Hey. I couldn't help but overhear you—but the whole room couldn't help but overhear."

Lolly jerked straight, her head swiveling to Vicky. The door slipped out of her hand, shutting slowly behind.

The mob hushed. Vicky could feel the weight of all eyes on her. Her inner lion froze.

Slo-mo, Lolly's gaze dropped to where Vicky held her. Vicky's heart leaped up to beat in her throat. Lolly's eyes, glittering with malice, rose and locked with Vicky's.

Vicky dropped her hand.

Lolly gave her a disdainful once-over. Then turned away, nose in the air.

"Ooh, the cut direct," Vicky murmured. It was so overdone that Vicky's doubts and hesitation fled.

She raised her voice. "The official staff at this door has asked you for your ticket, ma'am. She'd like to see it, and frankly, I think all these people waiting patiently in line would like to see it too."

Lolly stiffened. Then, with a sniff, she spun from the door and stalked away.

"Good job," Ronnie said.

"Thanks." Vicky watched Lolly stomp away like a spoiled little girl.

"Not so good for you though. Now you're in the crosshairs of the Dragon's hate radar."

* * *

Zan came upon the sisters just in time to see Lolly Darling stomp away. Taking in the crowd, seeing the angry expressions as affronted stares followed Lolly, the stressed pale face of young woman staffing the ticket table, Ronnie's raised brow, and Vicky's slim body trembling with anger, and he knew the story behind the scene. *Good for you, Dr. Brooks.*

He was considering his approach when Ronnie moved off toward the restrooms, Vicky waving goodbye.

Heading straight for Vicky, he called, "Ronnie" with no volume at all. Hey, he'd been a professor. He could bellow loud enough to subdue a lecture hall of eight hundred if he needed to. "Ronnie, wait." He stopped—coincidentally right next to Vicky—and frowned, putting his hands on his hips, as if in consternation. "Darn. Missed her."

Then he turned to Vicky. Smiled expectantly at her. "Hi."

"Hi." A delicious pink blush rode her cheeks.

He found he wanted to kiss that pink skin. "I'm Zan Sinclair. You're Vicky Brooks? I'm acquainted with your sister."

"I know." Her voice was breathy, oh-so-sexy. "She said."

Her lips were a perfect natural rose. He wondered if they'd be petal soft if he kissed them....

"I'll go get her for you!" Vicky scooted off.

Lost in her lips, he was totally unprepared for her flight. He stood there in surprise. He was wondering what he should do now when she trotted back with her sister in tow.

Ronnie didn't look happy until she caught sight of him. Then her whole face changed, and she hove out in front of her twin like a barge.

And Vicky...stopped. She began to turn. He clenched fists. She was going to run away *again*. He had only seconds to act or lose her.

He covered the distance in two strides, catching Ronnie by the upper arm with one hand and Vicky by the shoulder with the other.

Her slight body was warm and soft under his fingers. A distracting surge of sheer need flooded his system. She looked up into his face, her eyes big and blue.

Her pouty pink lips trembled.

His whole body hardened, instantly ready. He almost ignored the people milling around them to yank her to him, to feel her heart flutter against him, to embrace her, to *kiss* her...

"Alex, what's so important that it won't wait for me to freshen up?" Ronnie tapped his chest playfully.

He released them both with a silent groan. "I wanted to let you know..." Vicky's toes were turning away so he added quickly, "I wanted you *both* to know I've planned a get-together this evening with Winters." Vicky stopped, her gaze rising shyly. "I wanted a chance for the four of us to get to know each other better before the Gala." His words were aimed at Ronnie, but his eyes were tangled with Vicky's. They really were the prettiest blue...

"Good idea!" Ronnie said. "Vicky's been looking forward to meeting her date. She got a dress, you know, and I found a darling little pair of shoes..."

While Ronnie was talking, Vicky's fingers fluttered toward her shoulder where he'd held her for that brief moment. Her eyes were still locked with his, her expression awed.

He knew what that gesture meant and nearly crowed in triumph.

She had enjoyed his touch.

Her fingers stopped. He could see the exact instant she realized she'd betrayed herself. Her lashes fluttered down to shutter her gaze.

She was about to run off *again*. Leaving him alone in Ronnie's clutches. *Not.* He reached out.

Even before he moved, she blurted, "Good grief, why am I standing here, horning in? You two will want to be alone. To, um, catch up on things." Blushing a rosy red, she spun and left.

CHAPTER FIVE

Zan rode the stationary bicycle in his penthouse suite so fast he was surprised the carpet didn't smoke. He'd left the crowded hallway immediately after Vicky, not even waiting a decent interval, too frustrated to pretend to be civil. Ronnie had called after him with that hurt little catch in her voice that she'd perfected. But she still had his credit card. Whatever hurt she imagined he'd dealt her, a good round of shopping on his chit would make up for it.

Normally he went out of his way not to be rude. But his emotions, usually glass-lake-still, had flared out of control, pushing him to get away. Once he'd reached the coolness of his rooms, he'd gotten his feelings in hand, gotten his intellect online, and texted Ronnie an apology for running off. Then he started trying to figure out what to do about this latest setback. What a giant FUBAR.

Vicky had run from him because she thought he wanted time alone with *Ronnie*. Probably why she'd disappeared the first time. She was leaving him clear for her sister.

He stopped pedaling as a horrible follow-up thought struck him. What if she believed he'd attended the conference *because* of her sister?

What if Ronnie believe that, too?

Crap, what had he done? He'd texted Ronnie to get her here but hadn't fully considered what spin

Ronnie might have put on his words. He yanked his phone from his workout pants, pulled up the text, and reread it from Ronnie's point of view. Double crap with a side of damn. Not quite casual enough. Ronnie's personal worldview cast herself as the sun. She probably even thought the whole convention was an excuse to get back together with her.

He shoved his phone back in his pocket and started pedaling again. Bad enough, but there was worse.

He hadn't missed Ronnie's words when he'd proposed the get-together tonight. "Vicky's been looking forward to meeting her date."

His ploy to use Nate Winters to deflect Ronnie's jealousy while he got acquainted with Vicky had backfired, big-time. Now both sisters were convinced Nate was for Vicky and he was for Ronnie.

This was a mess. Zan stopped pedaling to dig a hand into his hair. A mess, and his own fault. He hated when that happened.

His mess. Up to him to clean it up.

Right. A few solid deep breaths calmed him. Analyze the situation. Come up with a plan. He could do this.

At least he and Vicky had finally officially met. A smile lifted his lips. Those few words, the brief touches, only made him more eager to know her better. In fact, the slivers of time he'd spent in her presence, hearing her sweet voice, seeing her delicious pink blush, smelling her light feminine scent...

Oh, he wanted to get to know her better, all right. The tightening in his groin told him just how much better.

He left the machine to take a cold shower.

The mix-up meant his original plan was out. A friendly get-together with Ronnie and Vicky, gradually working Ronnie *out*, wasn't going to fly with both sisters doing their darnedest to keep Ronnie *in*.

At least Ronnie's emotions weren't on the line. From her behavior...an expensive lunch, shopping on his credit card, sitting at the head table...oh, yes, she was more interested in the trappings of billionaire Dr. Sinclair than Zan himself. Ronnie wouldn't be heartbroken that he wasn't interested in her romantically.

He got out of the shower and briskly dried off.

Somehow he had to convince Vicky, too. From her reaction, she believed it much more strongly than Ronnie.

Well, tackle the easier task first. Nate Winters could distract Ronnie, although it might be harder now that she had Zan as her agenda. To distract a focused Ronnie...he shuddered slightly. That would take a little more effort.

Thank goodness Nate owed him big-time.

Before *Revealing Secrets*, when Zan's star had yet to go nova, Nate was already famous for teaching emotional communications to actors. Celebrities from all over the globe learned verbal and nonverbal techniques to convey real emotions from Nate; he was called the Feelings Doc.

So when society maven Leda Loper invited Zan to his first big charity event, he'd watched Nate closely for cues how to behave. He'd never forgotten what happened to famous men who attended events solo.

"There he is!"

The moment Nate had stepped over the sill, a crush of women, faces from eager to hungry, had nearly taken him to the floor of the elegant mansion.

Zan's swift action, leaping in, yanking Nate out by the collar and hauling him away, had saved Nate from being trampled. That incident, plus Nate's marriage fiasco with the heiress, meant Nate still owed him.

For a moment, Zan felt bad. Nate wasn't any more interested in a long-term relationship than Zan had been. But Nate's romancing Ronnie, if only through the Feelings Doc appealing to her actor side, was the only way Zan could think of to have a chance to spend time with Vicky.

Hopefully it'd be enough.

* * *

Vicky tugged at the crayon-yellow dress, trying to avoid her reflection in the gold-veined, mirrored panels beside the elevator. Waiting was always more painful when you looked like a pregnant lemon.

"Stop that," Ronnie murmured, checking her makeup in the mirrors. The supermodel's rich copper eye shadow and sleek black liner made the green of her contacts even more striking. Blush accentuated her strong cheekbones, and powder gave her flawless skin a finished look. A red hourglass dress hugged every delectable curve. Tonight, Ronnie Rivers was beyond gorgeous.

Unlike Vicky Brooks, who now knew what a rooster in a sock felt like. "Ronnie, this is your dress. It's made for you. It *likes* you—and it hates me." The bosom gaped like she was two coconuts shy of a tree. To make up for it, the skirt was so tight across her hips that, no matter how many times she tugged it down, it kept riding back up. The yellow washed her complexion so sallow she appeared to have terminal jaundice. When she closed her lids, the pale pink eye shadow Ronnie had insisted she use was the height of zombie chic.

"It's my third-best dress." Ronnie pulled a tube of gloss from her tiny purse and slicked another layer on her plump lips. "More importantly, it's the only dress I had that vaguely fits you. Don't worry. With that short skirt and those pencil heels? Your legs look good. Nobody will be looking at any of the other stuff."

"I don't think the skirt's supposed to be quite this short." Vicky tugged it down again. The instant she let go, it promptly rode up her hips like a window shade retracting. "And trying to walk in these heels is an invitation to the ER."

"Chill." Ronnie rolled her eyes, with a smile to soften it. "It's not like this is a formal occasion."

Vicky clung to that. Besides, the deadly heels did make her legs look good. "Where are we meeting them again?"

"*Not* Alex's penthouse suite." Ronnie pouted and put her gloss away. "I did try to convince him when he phoned with the time and place."

"Too bad," Vicky lied. Having drinks with Zan Sinclair was scary enough. Drinks in his private suite, his bedroom nearby, with his *bed*? That would've been enough to give Vicky terminal hot flashes. "So where, then?"

"The Coliseum. Three bars, plus a live band for dancing."

"Lovely for talking." Vicky's turn to roll her eyes. Not that she'd thought to stun either Sinclair or Winters with her scintillating conversation, but she had counted on listening to *them* talk. Over the pounding of a live band? Her lip-reading skills were minimal. She wondered if there was an app for that yet.

"Alex will have reserved a private alcove," Ronnie said as the elevator dinged.

The doors opened and they got on. Vicky's nerves and the unaccustomed high heels made her stumble across the threshold.

Ronnie caught her, a flash of concern lighting her face. "Are you okay?"

Flushing, Vicky straightened. "Yes, of course."

"Victoria Emma Brooks. You're nervous, aren't you?" Ronnie raised a brow as the doors shut and the elevator started up. "Is Nate Winters *that* cute?"

It was as good an excuse as any. Ronnie would never understand the real reason. "Very handsome. And smart."

"Rich?"

"That too."

"Hmm." Ronnie tapped a finger against her chin.

"Hmm, what?"

"Just considering my options. If, you know, Alex doesn't work out."

"What? Hey." The wash of consternation overcame Vicky's nerves. She crossed her arms. "You get one or the other. You don't get *both.*"

"Whoa, cowgirl." Ronnie grinned. "You get Nate. I'll keep my hands off—tonight. But later...well, you don't live in California. You can't actually keep him."

Vicky slumped. That was too true, for both Winters and Sinclair.

A ding announced their arrival at the club level. The elevator doors slid open to a long, dark hallway throbbing to a heartbeat of drums and flashing lights.

"Come on." Ronnie danced out of the elevator. "This will be fu-un."

Getting drunk and acting like an idiot in front of Zan Sinclair and Nathaniel Winters, the two biggest names in communications. Just Vicky's idea of fu-un.

Gaze following her sister, she frowned. What *would* she consider really fun?

Well...sitting down with the men, discussing their latest books, maybe with a frothy mocha or thick wedge of pie...yes, that would be fun.

Wingman. This wasn't for her. It was for Ronnie. Vicky dug deep into her well of patience and strength and stepped out of the elevator.

And tripped, nearly splitting the skirt of the yellow dress as she caught herself. It did ride up to her panty line. Cheeks boiling, she tugged it down.

Snicker.

Her head snapped up. A long, long line of people milled in the hallway outside the Coliseum. At her end was a young woman whose hand inadequately covered a wide grin.

Lovely. Who *hadn't* seen her wardrobe malfunction?

"Stop dawdling, Vicky." Ronnie came back and grabbed her hand. "I'd like to see the boys sometime tonight." She pulled Vicky past the line of people, seemingly oblivious to the darkening scowls and mutters of "line jumper".

But those glares hit Vicky's guilt gland dead center, especially remembering Lolly Darling's rudeness. This was different, because they were meeting Winters and Sinclair, but Vicky wondered if she'd ever feel comfortable with privilege. She got more and more self-conscious as she stumbled after her sister until, by the time they reached the club, she was ready to apologize to everyone and anyone. She swallowed nervously. "Sorry," she said to the nearest glowering woman.

"Ass," the woman snarled.

"Here we are." Ronnie finally let go. A single unmarked glass door, apparently the club entrance, was guarded by a burly man. He wasn't letting anyone through, and he was big enough that nobody was arguing.

He held up a hand as Ronnie danced into range.

Vicky wiped damp palms on the skirt of the dress, streaking it with perspiration.

Ronnie tickled the air with her fingertips, motioning the doorman to lean toward her. She said something in his ear.

The burly man nodded. He straightened and rapped on the door.

A young, shapely woman in an old-fashioned movie usherette's uniform came to the glass. No skirt riding up for her, and she stood confidently on platform heels taller than Vicky's.

Although the usher's heels had cute herringbone spats.

Vicky briefly scrunched her eyes. Assassin heels, okay because they were cute.

The usher raised a questioning brow at the bouncer. He pointed up. Her other brow winged high.

He opened the door. Ronnie sailed through.

"Welcome, ladies." The usher waved Ronnie in with white-gloved hands as if she were directing air traffic. Ronnie sauntered past her with an extra swagger to her hips.

Vicky followed more cautiously. She stepped into pulsing music, flashes of a light show, and bursts of laughter. Staff breezed past with trays, not beer and peanuts but fancy cocktails and square plates of pretty hors d'oeuvres. The rich scent of expensive cologne and perfumes wafted from the laser-studded dark.

This wasn't a bowling alley in St. Louis on a Saturday night. This was a haven of the elite.

Good heavens. What was she, plain Vicky Brooks, doing here? She wasn't a socialite, wasn't great fun at parties, and wasn't even a bizarre but interesting conversation starter.

Heart thudding painfully, Vicky nearly turned tail to run. She wasn't in the same social set or even the same universe as her sister, Winters, and Sinclair. Hell, she wasn't in even the same reality. She cut a glance behind her, wondering how far away the elevator and escape was...

The corridor was lined with black stares. *Line jumper.*

She flinched.

Damn it, no. She wasn't here for herself, she was here for her sister. No chickening out allowed.

She'd already taken another step into the club when a hand clamped on her wrist, amazingly strong.

"Come *on.*" Ronnie pulled her through the dark after the usher.

They caught up to the woman as she reached a glittering gold-and-glass elevator. Smiling at them, she unlocked the elevator with a gold key. Ronnie released Vicky to dance in. Vicky squared her shoulders and followed. The contraption drew them smoothly up to a floor that was much quieter, cooler, and darker.

Vicky stepped out with a sigh of relief. She took a few steps to a handrail and looked down. She stood on a balcony ringing the second floor, the main floor exposed below.

Behind her, the usher strutted off on her heels, Ronnie following. Vicky spun and, keeping a hand on the rail for balance, scurried after.

The balcony's curved wall was punctuated by a dozen arches curtained in red velvet. Five sets of curtains were tied back, revealing large alcoves. Semicircular banquettes of red leather lined each alcove, seating for the big, round tables dressed in red and black woven silk. One had the remains of a meal and several drinks on it.

The usher led Ronnie and Vicky to one of the closed alcoves. She knocked on the wall next to the alcove, turned, and swept a hand toward its red curtains.

Vicky froze. That hand, held out, meant they were supposed to do...something. Damn it, she was a communications expert, knew enough social scripts and cues to ace any standardized test.

But she had no idea what the usher wanted from her.

Ronnie, thank goodness, parted the velvet eagerly. The usher gave them a brief, almost awed bow and left, her herringbone-covered heels flashing. Vicky watched her go, then turned. Time to get this over with.

In those few seconds, Ronnie had shimmied through the gap and disappeared, and the curtains had swung closed.

Vicky's heart tripped. She lurched forward, hand extended, trying to remember the location of the opening, certain she'd have to dig through folds like a panicked actress trying to escape the stage.

She stumbled over her heels. Her fingers clutched the curtain, trying to catch her balance. The rod wasn't strong enough to hold her plummeting weight. She wrenched the curtain down, bending the rod. A gap sprang open at the top of the arch, mellow candlelight glowing through.

Vicky got her feet under her then stumbled again, cheeks burning hot, just as the curtain parted.

Zan Sinclair stood there.

"You're right, the red velvet is pretentious." His lips were curved. "The curtains, I mean. But it's the only way to get privacy. Come in." He held the velvet open for her.

She wanted to melt into liquid and dribble off the balcony. She ducked her head and hurried to sit— only to trip yet again.

This time strong hands caught her shoulders. *Zan.* "Careful," he murmured, his dark, potent male voice *right* in her ear. "There's a step."

Of course there was. The booth was raised, and she'd missed it. Liquid? Embarrassment would flame her straight to gas.

Cursing the unaccustomed heels no matter how long they made her legs look, she managed to stumble onto the riser with the help of Zan's strong hands. This close, this real, she couldn't think of him as Sinclair. She slid onto the nearest corner of the banquette, nine o'clock if the archway was six. She stuffed her little purse in her lap, stared at it, and concentrated on dissolving into as small a puddle of unnoticed goo on the seat as she could.

From the corner of her eye, she saw her sister's leg in the ten o'clock position—all of her leg. Ronnie's slide had hiked her skirt to the lacy tops of her thigh-highs. "Ronnie," Vicky whispered. "Your skirt—"

"Hi." Ronnie stuck out her hand to the man sitting at twelve. "I'm Ronnie Rivers, the actress. You must be Nate Winters. I've heard so much about you."

"And I, you." Dr. Nathaniel Winters smiled and took Ronnie's hand—and Vicky's breath. In his pictures, he was handsome; in person, his lips had a decidedly sensuous curl that made her tummy buzz. He leaned into Ronnie and kissed the air by both of her cheeks.

Ronnie laughed the bell-like trill she'd perfected in junior high. "You've heard good things, I hope."

"Of course." Winters switched his grip and brought Ronnie's manicured fingers up to his lips. Kissed the tips. "I've heard only beautiful things about a beautiful lady."

Watching this interplay, Vicky was unprepared for a significant weight denting the seat beside her, and she rolled into a hard, warm body. A long, muscular thigh pressed along the length of hers...it was Sinclair. Gasping, she scooted over to make room.

She hit Ronnie. Ronnie's hand speared Winters's mouth. He jerked back.

"Sorry," Vicky spluttered. "I'm so sorry!"

"No harm done," Winters said, blood welling on his upper lip. Ronnie's nails were long, sharp, and wickedly strong. The blood started trickling. Winters tested the tear with his tongue. "Or not much."

Ronnie *tsked*. "Oh, look how we're all crowded together. Alex, go sit over there." She pointed at the banquette opposite her, at the three o'clock position. "Vicky, slide out for a moment."

Sinclair raised one black brow but dutifully backed off the banquette and went to sit on the other side. Vicky started to slide out.

Before she could stand, Sinclair caught her eye.

And patted the red leather next to him.

Vicky froze, the air in her lungs evaporating. Dr. Alexander Sinclair wanted *her* to sit next to him?

"Move it, Sis." Ronnie nudged Vicky out of the banquette. Vicky stumbled to her feet while Ronnie slid out behind her.

Then Ronnie dropped gracefully into the space Sinclair had indicated.

Vicky briefly clenched her eyes. She'd been indulging in fantasy again. Sinclair wanted *Ronnie* to sit next to him. Not Vicky in her lemon tube-sock of a dress.

Except against her closed lids, an after-image of Sinclair's face showed a micro-expression—a flash expression, impossible to fake.

His face bore a tiny, almost imperceptible, sour frown.

And what that expression implied...Vicky's eyes sprang wide open as her legs trembled and went out from under her, dumping her onto red leather. Sinclair didn't want Ronnie sitting next to him.

He *had* been looking at her.

No, ridiculous. How could she think that? Sinclair had texted *Ronnie* to meet him at the convention. He'd called *Ronnie* to set up this meet. He'd given *Ronnie* his credit card for the Gala.

For Vicky's dress.

Perched on her corner of the banquette, she tried to make sense of any of it.

"So, Alex." Ronnie turned brightly to Sinclair. "Did the *Revealing Secrets* producer happen to come to the convention? I'd love to meet him."

"Hi." The famous whiskey-smooth baritone of Dr. Nate Winters sounded in Vicky's ear. She looked up. He'd slid from the twelve o'clock position to nine, and she'd effectively been snubbing him.

"I'm sorry," she blurted. To try to make amends, she speared out her hand. "I'm Vicky Brooks."

Winters flinched.

Her cheeks fired again. What about these famous, suave men made her act like a rampaging toddler? She started to withdraw her hand.

He snared it before she could. When he had her fingers securely in his, he said, "Nice to meet you, Vicky Brooks. *Dr.* Brooks, isn't it? You're in communications like Zan and me."

His hand was warm, his grasp firm. Answering heat rose throughout her body. "Why...yes. How did you know?"

"Zan told me."

Alexander Sinclair knew she was in communications? How? It didn't seem the sort of thing that would come up in idle conversation with Ronnie.

Although, *duh.* This was a communications convention. What else would she be? Not an actress, not with her looks.

A rap sounded outside the closed curtains. A moment later, they rustled and parted, and a waitress in short shorts and a sequined demi top spun a tray onto their table. "Whiskey for the gentlemen." She set short glasses of golden and amber liquid before Sinclair and Winters. "S'mores for the ladies." Tall tulip glasses were placed before her and Ronnie, filled with alternate swirls of chocolate brown, graham cracker tan, and cream white. Long-handled teaspoons went onto the table next to them. "Enjoy." The waitress grinned and left, the curtains swishing closed behind her.

"What's this?" Ronnie tapped the glass with one fingernail.

"Taste it," Winters urged. "It's something Sinclair and I invented."

She dipped the spoon into the glass. Her tongue darted out like a pretty pink butterfly and touched the chocolate and white confection. Then she turned a huge smile on Sinclair. "Alex, you naughty man. You know I have to watch my figure so that my dress fits for the Gala." But her trill of laughter said she wasn't upset at all.

Vicky took her own spoon, dipped up a mound, and thrust it into her mouth with much less charm.

Flavors hit her tongue. Chocolate ice cream. Marshmallow cream. Graham cracker powder. And the buzz of chocolate liqueur. "This is *wonderful.*"

Sinclair's eyes turned to her, and they were warm and crinkled at the corners, as if he liked seeing her satisfied. "I hoped you'd enjoy it."

That almost-smile would be on his face as he pleasured a woman. Intimately.

She dropped her spoon. Swallowed hard. "Um, well, thanks for ordering it for me...I mean us." She hoped her flash of desire wasn't evident on her face.

His eyes darkened. Okay, apparently it was evident, very evident.

But more—he liked it.

Vicky's whole body went up in flames. *Poof.*

Ronnie cleared her throat. Vicky's gaze shied away from hot, dark eyes...to meet shooting green flames. Ronnie was seeing Vicky's *me want* too.

Vicky's cheeks rushed with heat like a furnace had kicked in.

"Dr. Winters!" She turned to him. "Thank you. Also. Thanks for the drink, Dr. Winters."

"Call me Nate, please." There was a chuckle in his voice, as if he'd caught the interplay.

Well, of course he had. His specialty was emotional communication. He'd have caught every mortifying nuance.

Vicky's flush of heat was replaced by ice. She had to escape. *Now.* "Um, I'll just..." She waved at the closed curtains. "I've got to, um, you know." She rose. Her feet were blocks of ice. She took a single step and had to grab the table for balance.

"Do you know where the ladies' room is?" Winters voice came urbanely from behind her.

"I'll find it." She nodded, more to get the blood flowing in her brain than as a yes. "I think. I hope."

"Oh, for heaven's sake. I'll go with you." Ronnie's disgust radiated as she slid out from her side of the banquette. "Come on." She pulled aside the far end of the curtain.

Vicky tried to follow Ronnie out. She took a step away from the table, toward where her sister was gracefully exiting.

She misjudged the size of the table and caught the edge with her hip. Her legs, already wobbly, started to fold on her. She managed to stick one foot out to brace herself, but her momentum pitched her over her own leg, and she flew headlong toward the floor.

Sinclair half-rose, directly in her path. Strong hands snared her just as she barreled into him. Her momentum pushed them back onto the banquette.

Somehow she ended up a tangle of limbs—on his lap.

CHAPTER SIX

Large, warm hands righted her. Vicky sat for a moment on oaken male thighs, simply getting her breath back. Palms burned through the yellow dress, branding her ribs.

Good heavens. She was in *Zan's* lap. His legs were under hers, his muscled torso pressed against her side. Her mouth was level with his...her body burned. Mortified, she wiggled to get off him.

His hands tightened. The dress was slippery, and her wriggling slid his hand smack into the undercurve of her breast.

A breast that suddenly was stiff and full. She squeaked. "I...I'm sorry."

"Don't apologize," he growled. His eyes were very dark indeed, pupils fully dilated. She could see the brush of individual hairs in his eyebrows, the long, thick lashes...

The curtain opened again. "Well? What are you waiting for—?"

Vicky swiveled to see Ronnie's face morph from annoyed to stunned. Vicky blinked rapidly, trying to think of what she should be saying, what she should be doing.

All she could think of was how amazing Sinclair's hands felt on her body.

"Oh, get up," Ronnie snarled, grabbing Vicky's wrist and yanking her to her feet. Off Sinclair's lap. Off the strength of Sinclair's muscular thighs... Ronnie hauled her away from the booth and around the balcony toward a hallway.

"Wish I'd thought of that," Ronnie said as she pushed into a gilt restroom. "But don't do it again. Ever."

Vicky swallowed hard. "I'll try not to."

* * *

As the curtains fluttered shut, Zan shifted on the red leather banquette, trying to find a comfortable position. The feel of Vicky's sleek, soft body under his palms, the smell of her filling his nose, had thundered straight through him until his blood roared. Her lush backside, wiggling against him, had turned his body so hard he thought he'd burst from his pants.

"That was interesting," Nate said brightly from across the table. "Do you think she did it on purpose?"

Zan growled. "No."

Nate laughed. "I agree. But the way it's wound your shorts, she couldn't have been any more effective if she had."

"She didn't. She doesn't even know I'm interested."

"Oh, please," Nate said. "How can she not? You're more obvious than a horny teen wearing a big red button for a belt buckle."

"She thinks I'm angling for her sister." Zan told his friend about the mix-up.

"And you're supposed to be a communications genius." Nate *tsked*. Only Nate could make the sound so sarcastic.

"I'm off my game, all right? She's knocked me a bit sideways."

Nate grinned. "The cool Zan Sinclair, the great communicator—clogged up by emotions?" He took a swig of his drink. "*Burn.*"

Zan knew Nate wasn't talking about the whiskey. "It's not my fault. I'm so damned attracted to her." He shifted on the seat again. "Every time I see her, it gets exponentially worse. It's made hash of my control."

Nate's smile faded, his gaze becoming speculative. "How the mighty have fallen."

"I haven't fallen." Zan growled again. "Yet."

"Well, if Ms. Ronnie Rivers has any say, you won't ever, unless you topple in her direction. Why the hell did you involve her?"

Zan's growl died. "So she wouldn't feel cut out. Wouldn't take out her frustrations on Vicky. But Vicky keeps clearing the way for her sister."

"And that's stopping you, why? Wait until Vicky's alone."

"I did. She just ran off to get Ronnie."

Nate laughed. "You must have it bad. Normally you'd be in complete control of a situation. You idiot. Just do something so boring Ronnie won't *want* to be with you."

Zan blinked. "Sometimes, you're almost as smart as you think you are."

"You have a plan?"

"And a backup." He took out his smartphone.

"That's more like the Zan I know."

Zan smiled.

* * *

The next morning, Zan put his plan into motion, waiting for Vicky with a trick up his sleeve.

Or actually, a couple tickets in his pocket.

He felt bad about working around Ronnie. But last night, when the women had returned, Ronnie had smiled brightly at him through freshly applied lipstick, grabbed the space next to him with a proprietary slide, and pressed every inch of her body against him. He'd disengaged her gently but frankly didn't want to deal with her this morning.

His desperation was exacerbated by the fact that, when Vicky had slid in next to Nate, even the foot of airspace she'd kept between them had felt too close for Zan. The instant need for a woman he'd never met, the exponential growth of desire with each glimpse or word, and now him, proprietary about a woman? Unbelievable. He needed to get to the bottom of it fast.

Which meant getting to know Vicky better, right? Right.

He'd timed it carefully, waiting until just before Nate's morning session, a highly technical treatment of nonverbal communications. Vicky had gone into a lecture room while Ronnie flit off toward the shops. Vicky was alone.

She stood just inside the room, eyeing up the choice of seats. He rushed in, hoping she wouldn't run away until he'd made his plea.

He did give her a slight warning. "Dr. Brooks. Vicky!" He clasped her shoulder.

She jumped under his hand. Swiveled to look up at him over her shoulder.

She really had the brightest blue eyes, the sweetest pink lips. After the initial surprise, her lips curved in a real smile, which reassured him to no end.

"Oh, Dr. Sinclair! You startled me."

"Sorry about that. And call me Zan, please."

"Oh." Her cheeks pinked to the same shade as her lips. "I don't know if I can. You're the biggest name in the field. You're...you."

He got distracted for an instant with the insane need to coax his name from her pretty petal lips. But he really had only left himself a few moments to win her over. He started his pitch. "I'm glad I ran into you. I have a couple tickets to Winters's session in the Grand Ballroom."

That caught her attention. "But it's sold out."

"Yes. Nate gave me comps. I hate to go to these things alone. Come with me?"

Her eyes lit with pleasure. Then she closed them and shook her head. "You'll want Ronnie. I'll go get her."

She was going to run away *again*. But this time Zan was smart. He hadn't let go of her shoulder. As she turned, his fingers tightened. She stopped, obviously surprised and confused. He said quickly, "No time! Winters goes on in two minutes. We'll miss the talk. *I'll* miss the talk unless you come now."

She turned back slowly.

He watched her carefully for her real reaction. If she looked at his hand on her shoulder first, then she wanted him to release her and didn't want to accompany him. But if she looked at *him...*

Her eyes lifted to his, and it stole his breath. They were a gut-wrenching mix of hope, guilt, and longing. She said, with a hesitation that tugged at his heart, "You want *me* to go with you?"

"Yes." It was all he could do to keep from howling his triumph. "Very much."

"Well..." She glanced at the doorway where her sister had sashayed away moments before. "I'm not Ronnie."

He was so anxious to convince her he said, "This is Winters's technical presentation. It's not acting. Ronnie wouldn't enjoy it."

He knew it was a mistake the instant it left his mouth.

"She wouldn't, would she?" Vicky nodded as if that cleared things up. "Of course you'd want me to go, since Ronnie would be bored." As if only Ronnie's feelings on the matter counted.

Zan couldn't let her keep that impression. "That's not why—"

"I've been wanting to go." She turned toward him. "Wishing I could go. But it was sold out before I even heard it was added. Dr. Winters is supposed to be an incredibly charismatic speaker."

Zan's gut suddenly churned with something viciously close to jealousy. It took all his concentration to push the feeling away. Nate was one of his best friends. Emphasis on *was*. "Yes. He's a great speaker. So you'll come?"

"Gladly."

She finally came willingly with him, a smile on her face. But she was willing because she thought her sister wouldn't want to go. And the smile was put there by his ex-friend Nate.

Zan had won the battle, but the cost was almost too high, and the war was far from over.

* * *

Zan ushered Vicky into the roped-off seats of the front row, keeping his hand firmly on her arm, ostensibly to guide her, but in truth, he liked touching her. He was having a hard time reining in the impulse to brush her hair back from her face or to put his arm around her. To kiss her.

Baby steps. He was finally alone with her.

Alone...if you didn't count their several hundred colleagues, applauding loudly as Winters took the platform stage. But Vicky was here, sitting next to him, without her sister.

Baby steps.

Then she pulled subtly away from him, putting the same breadth of space between them as she had between her and Winters last night.

That threw him into a state of agitation. What did *that* mean? Was she disgusted by him? Attracted to Nate? Just adopting a neutral space? Even neutral thrust a spear into his heart.

Winters started with his usual joke. While the audience erupted in laughter, Vicky turned to Zan and smiled.

His insides eased. He smiled back.

At his smile, hers disappeared, her eyes widened, and she turned her attention immediately back to Winters.

And just what the hell did *that* mean? Had she seen his attraction in his eyes and been disgusted? Frightened? Or had she liked his smile but was so unsure of herself that she'd thought he'd read her attraction and was embarrassed...? Damn it, he could spin a dozen possibilities but wasn't sure about any of them. Nate was right, he was a mess around her. He'd always kept himself free of muddling emotion just because of this. He'd never been so rattled around anyone before, and he wasn't sure he liked it.

But sitting next to her...warmth flooded him, and not just his groin. Okay, he didn't like muddling emotion, but he liked this. He liked being with her, smelling her, touching her. He liked it a lot.

He shifted in his chair to brush his sleeve against her arm.

A second of golden perfection.

Then she contracted, putting a centimeter of air between them.

It kicked him in the solar plexus. Damn it, was she attracted to him or not? She was giving him mixed signals. Or signals he couldn't read. And he could read *anyone.*

Except now, when he was second-guessing and triple-guessing himself.

He hadn't been this communications-blind since seventh grade when he was a gangling idiot.

Automatically he retreated mentally. He'd do almost anything not to go back to that battered, misunderstood boy.

He'd retreated physically, too, judging by Vicky's startled glance. In reaction, she clasped her hands on her lap, pulled her elbows in, and turtled her head. Pulling inside herself too.

Oh, God. While he'd do almost anything not to get hurt again, it couldn't be at the cost of hurting *her*.

He straightened. Reached to touch her arm.

When she looked up at him, he smiled.

She didn't smile back.

He steeled himself against her rejection and rubbed his hand reassuringly along her arm. She was trembling. He took her tightly woven fingers in his own. Despite the heat of the packed crowd, her fingers were cold. He curled his fingers around hers more tightly.

She looked down at his hand covering hers then back up at him. There was a question in her eyes.

With all his second-guessing, he couldn't read exactly what the question was. But clearly she needed reassurance. So he smiled again at her and rubbed his thumb gently across the back of her hand.

The audience applauded at some point Winters had made. Vicky smiled tentatively at Zan. His chest burst with satisfaction bordering on joy, as if the applause was for him.

Her head tilted a question, her glossy brown hair falling forward over her shoulder. He couldn't answer the question, either by word or gesture. He was too full right now.

But she seemed to understand something in return. Because she unlaced her tightly clasped hands, slid one out from under his, and covered his hand with her own.

The sight of her slender fingers, so pale and small against the back of his hand, filled him with something else, something far richer. Hotter. He could feel the smile change on his face, become charged with his attraction.

Just as he saw a reporter he recognized from Hollywood point a smartphone at them.

* * *

Ronnie slapped the paper down on the table in front of Vicky. "What is this?"

Vicky groaned and wished she'd thought to make coffee before opening her hotel room door to Ronnie when she'd showed up at the unheard of hour of eight a.m.

It was the day after the lecture, and not starting well. As Vicky had let her sister in, one glance at Ronnie's storm-cloud face convinced Vicky she'd have to sit down for this. She'd led the way to the small table in the corner of her room and perched in one of the two chairs, inviting Ronnie to do the same. Ronnie had declined in order to pace angrily instead.

Now she jabbed the photo with a red nail, as if Vicky could miss it. "What the hell is this?"

After the lecture, Zan had mentioned the reporter but was swept off to an autograph session before he could explain. Her head full of Zan's smile, his touch, Vicky quickly forgot reporters. She'd gone to her various Friday lectures and workshops with wings for feet, daydreaming through most of them.

She'd remembered abruptly this morning, when she retrieved the complimentary newspaper deposited in front of her room's door. The moment she'd seen the photo, she knew she'd have to deal with Ronnie.

"This? Well...it's a picture of Dr. Sinclair. Communications expert to the stars? He's always a media target."

"That's not what I mean, and you know it."

Vicky did. The problem wasn't Sinclair. The problem was his expression, staring down at the

61

woman sitting next to him with such boiling desire that even she could see it.

That look was her most secret of fantasies, a dream come true.

Now it was a nightmare.

"You were supposed to be my *wingman,*" Ronnie spat. "Instead you steal my boyfriend out from under me!"

"It wasn't that way, Ronnie." Vicky was aware her tone was less emphatic than it should have been, because part of her hoped it *was* that way. And from Zan's face, it sure looked that way.

But Ronnie was upset, mad, and maybe even a little hurt. Vicky felt bad, and tried to soothe her. "Dr. Sinclair had two tickets to the presentation. He couldn't find you, so I went with him. No big deal. Anyway, it was a pretty technical lecture, Ronnie. You'd have been bored silly."

It was the wrong thing to say. She could *feel* her sister gather herself in outrage, didn't even have to see Ronnie's white nostrils or hear her sucked-in breath. "Bored silly? Bored *silly*? I'll have you know I went with Alex to an art show. And the symphony. I wasn't bored, and I wasn't silly!"

"No one suggested you were silly, Ronnie—"

"I am a sophisticated actor. I would have done my duty. No one would have known I wasn't riveted to every word."

Which implied she would have been utterly bored, as Zan had said. But Ronnie wasn't listening right now, so Vicky only said gently, "I'm sure that's true. But you weren't there and the lecture was starting—"

"And he was *my* date! And you stole him."

Vicky huffed a breath. What had she done that was so wrong? She hadn't meant to steal him, not intentionally. In fact, she hadn't done anything Ronnie hadn't done dozens of times to her. She'd just looked up into Zan's handsome face when he'd asked her to go to the lecture, and her heart had simply melted.

If she even had stolen him. She had doubts that Sinclair had truly tried to find Ronnie and had settled on Vicky by default.

She looked again at the photo. Talk about a picture saying a thousand words.

Except, couldn't photos be Photoshopped?

"Ronnie, look closer. I think this is all a mistake. You know those paparazzi will do anything to sell papers. The reporter caught Sinclair in the right light." She twisted the paper so his eyes didn't look quite so dark. "It only appears that he's looking 'that way' at me." She had another thought. "Sinclair probably wasn't even thinking about me. He just happened to be looking at me and was thinking about...about *you*. Probably." She smiled hopefully at her sister.

Ronnie frowned at the picture. "Well, maybe." Her expression cleared, and she gave a short laugh. "That's certainly a more likely explanation than that he's attracted to *you*."

"Ouch."

"Oh, you know I don't mean it that way." Ronnie's tone was abstracted. "You're probably right. It's just that...well, I came to the convention so happy, so full of expectations, and he's been so...distant." She gave a little hiccupping sob.

Vicky put her own needs away at the hurt tone in her sister's voice. "Oh, Ronnie. He'll call you...or text"—although come to think of it, what lover, hot to get back together, *texted* to get a date?— "and ask you to do something with him. And then things will be back on track."

"You think so?"

"I know so," Vicky said with more assurance than she felt.

"And he'll apologize." Ronnie tapped her chin thoughtfully. "Apologize charmingly. With a gift.

Flowers—or jewelry. Yes, for something like this, I think I'll hold out for jewelry."

"Um...isn't that a bit mercenary?"

Ronnie flashed her a startled look. "Of course not. I just know my own worth."

"But—"

"It's expected." Ronnie patted her shoulder. "That's how these things go at our level."

"Your *level?*"

"You know, like the peerage. The cement isn't feelings, which don't last, but money, which does. We join together for the good of the land, and a little sex—but not love."

Vicky's fingers curled in her lap. Zan's dark eyes, as he looked at her, had softened for a moment. She'd seen something in their depths—something vulnerable. Something that wasn't based on money but on those feelings that supposedly didn't last.

Strangely, Vicky got the idea that Ronnie might be able to hurt him. And suddenly she didn't want her sister, with her ideas of land, and a little sex—but not love—to have Zan Sinclair.

Which was ridiculous. Zan was immensely healthy and strong, both physically and emotionally. He was handsome and wealthy. Who could make him happier than Ronnie?

Just then, Ronnie's phone jangled a pop tune. A smile burst out on her face. "That's Alex. Looks like you were right." She grabbed her huge designer bag, a lumpy patchwork of crudely stitched-together scraps of leather, its sole distinction its famous name, and rummaged through it. The phone's ringtone was abruptly louder, cut off mid-cadence when Ronnie answered. "Hello, Alex dear...what?"

The deep male murmur was muffled by Ronnie's thick mane of hair. She turned away from Vicky to talk. Vicky couldn't hear what the man said, but she *could* read her sister's back quite clearly. Her spine neither stiffened nor folded. Not bad news, then.

"That's all right," Ronnie said. "I knew it wasn't intentional." More deep murmuring. Ronnie's spine softened, her hips cocking slightly. "I'd need to change clothes. How long?" A short murmur. "Yes. Looking forward to it, darling."

Vicky's stomach sank. The awaited reconciliation, complete with jewelry. She grabbed her elbows and waited for Ronnie to turn to her with the news that Sinclair had apologized and that he wanted to see Ronnie. At the last minute, she remembered to put on a brightly happy face.

CHAPTER SEVEN

But Ronnie just stood there. She stood there so long that Vicky felt her chest start to tingle. Oh, right, she wasn't breathing. She drew a breath and prompted, "Was that Dr. Sinclair?"

"Nate Winters, actually." Ronnie turned, and there was a thoughtful smile on her face. Vicky was surprised, both at the identity of the caller and the smile. "He said Alex was sorry the snap got in the paper and asked us to meet up with them to discuss what to do about it. He said to make sure you came." Ronnie gave her a pointed look.

"Me? Why...? Oh, you mean we'll make a foursome of it, in public, with me on Dr. Winters's arm and you with Dr. Sinclair, so the reporters get the right idea."

"Actually, no. We're meeting in Alex's penthouse. Half an hour. I'm going to change and freshen my makeup."

"His penthouse?" Vicky squeaked. That wasn't the plan. That wasn't being on Winters's arm in public. That was being in Zan's hotel room, just around the corner from Zan's *bed*. She put a hand to her breastbone; her heart was beating double-time at the very thought. "No, wait! I can't."

"Don't be silly. Of course you can. And you will." Ronnie dropped her phone into her bag and slung it over one shoulder. She managed to make the enormous, misshapen thing look stylish, but that was one of the many gifts Ronnie had. "Come to my room in half an hour. Don't be late."

"But we're supposed to *be* there in half an hour. If I come to your room in half an hour, that would make us both late..." Hearing herself babble, Vicky took a deep breath. She sounded panicked—which she was, but she didn't want to *sound* that way. "*If* I were going. Which I'm not."

"Of course you're going." Ronnie stared at her, the tiny lines between her eyes translating into a ferocious frown. "Why wouldn't you go?"

"Because...because I have the final fitting this morning. For my dress. For the Gala." She took another deep breath. Why wouldn't her rattling heart slow down? "The fitting is at ten, and I'd hate to rush the meeting."

Ronnie's mouth thinned. "Oh pooh. I guess I'll have to call Nate back and cancel." She dug in her bag.

"Wait, no. Why cancel? You can go."

"*Pfft.* Please. Who'll be with you at the fitting to make sure they haven't made your dress too tight? With your figure, you want to leave as much to the imagination as possible." She glanced up from her digging. "I didn't mean that the way it sounded."

"You never do," Vicky muttered, too anxious about the idea of being in Zan's room to guard her mouth.

"Hey. I didn't mean it. You know that."

Vicky winced.

Ronnie finally found her phone and thumbed in what appeared to be Redial. She put the phone to her ear. "Nate. It's Ronnie Rivers. We can't make it in half an hour. Vicky has a fitting for her Gala dress."

Vicky couldn't hear the deep reply, but Ronnie said, "Lovely. I'll wait for your call, then."

"What?" Vicky asked.

"Alex is making alternate arrangements. Nate will call back shortly."

"Shortly" turned out to be nearly twenty minutes. When the phone rang, Ronnie answered, then cooed, "Oh, that sounds wonderful. See you at one." As she ended the call, she turned to Vicky with a bright smile. "We're having lunch. At Rustermann's. Alex got a table—which is almost impossible on such short notice, let me tell you—and he'll have a taxi pick us up in front of the hotel at twelve-thirty. Come on, let's get to the dress shop."

"But my fitting isn't for another hour."

"Silly girl. We need to shop for new luncheon dresses now."

"Wait, what? I don't have money for a new dress."

"That's okay." Ronnie dimpled. "I still have Alex's credit card."

* * *

Zan had gone ahead of Nate to secure their private table upstairs at Rustermann's. It had cost him dearly to reserve the table on such short notice, but not as much as the expense of flying in his executive producer, Flynn Roberts, after figuring out the enormity of the fallout from that damned picture.

Totally worth it if he could maneuver a moment alone with Vicky.

He was done being subtle. Subtle had only gotten the wrong message to the wrong sister.

No, his goal today was to let Vicky know he was interested in *her*, not Ronnie. Hopefully Vicky felt the same interest in him. Then, very hopefully, between the two of them, they could find a way to ease Ronnie into that reality without triggering model meltdown.

He paced the private room, trying to keep his steps measured to control his tension. Emotions made for confused communications.

But it was hard not to feel both excitement and agitation. He was so close.

He glanced again at the clock. Nearly two. The women were now late by almost an hour. He glanced at the table where Nate sat with Flynn. The producer for *Secrets* was a gregarious, well-cushioned, bearded man, rather like a sandy-haired Santa Claus. He and Nate were comfortably talking and sipping their drinks. Zan paused in his pacing and took a deep breath, let it out over a long count. He had no doubt Vicky would have been on time, but Ronnie tended to prefer the dramatic entrance.

Sure enough, a full fifteen minutes later, Ronnie Rivers swept into the room, resplendent in a pink-and-green-flowered sarong, her blonde hair twisted up and pinned with carved jade sticks. "Alex!" She came at him, her arms spread with the intent of a full-body hug.

Zan neutralized that by catching her wrists and folding them together then air-kissing both cheeks. "Hello, Ronnie."

"Darling, it was so good of you to invite me to lunch."

Not *us?* He snapped eyes to the entrance. Vicky hovered hesitantly in the doorway. His heart rate slowed. "Hello, Vicky."

She gave him a trembling smile.

"I've ordered drinks for you, and appetizers. They should be here shortly." He kept one hand on Ronnie's wrist and reached out with the other to Vicky. "Let me introduce you both to Flynn."

Vicky advanced shyly into the room. He liked that about her, the sweet, unassuming way she moved. He caught her hand the moment she got in range and guided her gently toward the table. "Gentlemen, this is Ronnie Rivers and Dr. Vicky Brooks."

"The actress Ronnie Rivers," Ronnie said.

The men had risen. Zan said, "Ladies, you both know Nate. This other gentleman is Flynn Roberts. He's executive producer for my show."

"Mr. Roberts!" Ronnie yanked her wrist from Zan's grip and swept forward to Flynn, both hands out. "I've heard so much about you." She grabbed Flynn's offered hand with both of hers, leaned in, and puckered up.

At the last minute, Flynn turned his head so that her kiss landed on his cheek, awarding him with a smear of pink gloss. "Call me Flynn, please." Flynn straightened and tried to pull his hand away. He flashed a quick look at Zan over Ronnie's head. Zan knew whatever he'd already paid for flying Flynn here, it was nothing compared to what he was going to pay for this.

"Flynn, of course. You can call me Ronnie." She dimpled as she wedged herself between Flynn and Nate, pushing Flynn into his seat and nudging her backside into Nate's chair next to him.

Nate picked up his drink and moved one chair over, a wry smile on his face.

Normally Zan would have watched the interplay for the amusement value, but he had more important things on his mind. Ronnie was occupied with Flynn. Which left Zan with Vicky. He turned to her and took her hand in both of his. "Do you have a moment?"

She looked up at him, her oval face very serious. "Yes. I've been wanting to talk to you."

His insides thrilled. Then he saw the slight frown wrinkling her forehead. He chilled abruptly. He wasn't going to like this.

He drew her to a serving alcove off to the side of the room. While it was in partial view of the table, it was private enough for conversation. He wracked his brain as he led her there, trying to anticipate obstacles to his proposal.

So the minute they reached the alcove, he tried to sweep any possible objections away before she had a chance to establish them. "I'm sorry about that photo."

"I'm not."

It wasn't the response he'd expected. "You're not?"

"No. It made me see things more clearly."

He searched her face. She wasn't looking at him, and he was now certain he wasn't going to like this.

"You know, Ronnie thinks you invited her to this convention to get back together with her."

"I didn't mean that." He groaned inside. "It was a simple text message. She wasn't supposed to read anything into it."

"She's not in communications. CommuniCon wasn't something she would have attended otherwise. What else was she supposed to think?"

"That it was an opportunity for her to see her sister? Look, I can understand how she might have gotten the wrong impression. But it was *the wrong impression.*" He took both her hands in his and willed her to look at him. "It's not her I'm interested in."

She finally looked up into his eyes. Searched them. Read something in his gaze that made her whisper, "You must see it's impossible."

"I can assure you, it's not impossible at all." Just from the feel of her soft skin as his fingers laced with hers, hot lava poured through his veins. If she knew that, she'd understand just how *not* impossible it was.

"Dr. Sinclair...you must see that we're worlds apart."

"Worlds apart?" He jerked in surprise.

"But more, Ronnie has set her heart on you. She thinks you've gone beyond your three-date limit for her. That she's special to you." Pain shone in her eyes. "I won't be a party to hurting her."

"I didn't mean to hurt her." He said it about Ronnie, but with his gaze, he tried to tell her he hadn't meant to hurt *her*. "It wasn't supposed to be this way. It was a simple text." He couldn't keep the frustration out of his voice. "I thought the convention would be good for her. She wants to be an actress; the convention will be helpful."

"Don't you see, that's part of the problem?" She lowered her voice even more. "She *wants* to be an actress. She's trying to establish her next career option before modeling runs out—but she's not getting the bigger roles. She's not making the grade, and she knows it, so she's vulnerable right now. Don't you see what your reaching out to her means to her?"

"Oh God. I'm an imbecile." He shook his head. "At the time, it seemed simple enough. But I see it now." He closed his eyes briefly, clenching them against seeing all his plans, his hopes, slipping away.

If there was any way to salvage the situation, he had to be honest with her. Completely, utterly truthful.

Leaving himself open to misinterpretation and hurt.

But it had to be done.

"Vicky." He opened his eyes directly on hers and spilled it all. "I came here because I wanted to meet *you*. But I wanted to meet you in a way that Ronnie would still be involved, so she wouldn't feel like I was going behind her back. Surely I get points for considering Ronnie's feelings." He smiled at her, willed her to smile back.

But she was shaking her head. "It was good of you to think of her. But she got the wrong idea, and she's vulnerable. It's not your fault, but still."

Zan's insides crumpled. "You're not going to let me get to know you better?"

She did smile then, ruefully. "I'm Ronnie's wingman, so I'll be in your orbit. You're a communications genius. You'll know me better without even trying."

She disengaged her hands and went to sit next to Winters. Zan's eyes followed her.

The whole time they ate, he drank in the sight of her face. But she didn't look at him again, not once.

After it was over and everyone else was gone, Zan paid for the meal he hadn't even tasted.

* * *

"Ooh. I was afraid this Gala thing would be a boring old backwater shindig. But *look*." Ronnie's face glowed as she wheeled to take in all the glittering people in the huge ballroom.

Vicky smiled. She liked to see her sister have a good time, and this party promised to be one of the best. Ronnie fit right in, glittering too, with the subtle shine of her makeup and the gold lamé sheath that hugged her body like metallic plastic wrap.

"The Gala isn't just for communications wonks," Vicky said. "Everyone connected to the field attends. And this year, since we have Dr. Sinclair...well." The Gala had drawn people from throughout the country. Zan's presence had attracted the *crème de la crème*. "Did you want to get drinks?"

The open-bar reception was already underway. People lined up three and four deep at the several stations placed strategically around the edges of the ballroom. Others, standing with drinks in hand, chatted in small groups scattered throughout the room.

"Nah," Ronnie said. "I don't want my dress crushed. Let's find Alex and Nate and have them get us drinks." She glided into the center of the vast space that was dotted with a hundred tables dressed in frosty white linen set with gold-piped silverware and matching china. Though the topic of the convention was communications, the theme of the Gala was money, and it was evident in every aspect of the gathering.

Vicky followed, glad Ronnie was happily fitting in, because she herself had never felt so out of place, despite her gorgeous green gown. Ronnie moved through the throng as naturally as a swan diving into the water. Vicky was the duck waddling behind. She clasped her tiny purse in one hand and pretended it was a book. That made her feel a little better.

The silky material of her dress, sliding against her legs with each move, made her feel better still, a little more like she belonged.

Then, just for an instant, she lost sight of Ronnie. Her heart started racing. Her head flopped like a fish, trying to spot her sister or any familiar face in the crowd. Her heart rate, already high, spiked.

A flash of gold lamé caught her eyes. She sprinted for it, dodging gowned women and tuxedoed men. She caught up with Ronnie and seized her sister's gold-bangled wrist. Her heart rate slowed.

Ronnie eyed her strangely. "What's wrong with you?"

"Nothing." Everything. "Um...I haven't seen Dr. Winters and Dr. Sinclair. Are you sure they're here?"

"They have to be here." Ronnie's eyes suddenly lit up. "Oh, of course. They're probably in the greenroom, having drinks with the convention organizers. It's a thing."

Of course it was. Vicky knew all sorts of scripts on how to behave. But the ones that would be handy here, the rules for the rich and famous that Ronnie seemed to know instinctively, were a foreign language to Vicky. She felt like the actress in a bad dream who'd never even seen her lines, much less had time to memorize them. She clutched her purse harder, but it didn't miraculously turn into a book called *How to Be a Rich Bitch* or even *How to Feel a Little Less Awkward if You're Vicky Brooks.*

While she stood musing, Ronnie slid from her grip and glided off again.

Vicky broke into a trot to keep up. "Ronnie, wait!"

But Ronnie, moving effortlessly, didn't hear her.

Vicky gritted her teeth and accelerated until she was pumping along recklessly fast on her heels. She cursed tonight's insecurities, making her so clingy. She wasn't this needy in her own pond of the community college. There she was even a guide for the students. This behavior embarrassed her.

She gave herself a mental slap.

It jarred loose a thought. She was doing this wrong. She didn't have to keep up with Ronnie. All she had to do was *keep Ronnie with her,* which was easy. She just needed to get Ronnie talking.

She sprinted until she could snare her sister's arm. "Today at lunch. What did you and that producer talk about?"

"*Executive* producer." Ronnie stopped, thank goodness. "It was quite interesting. He's working on a pilot for a new show. A crime show, lots of sex and action. Not going to win any awards, but it'll be popular, which frankly interests me more."

"Popular?" Vicky kept a bright, inquisitive mask on her face while she gasped for breath. Lightheaded, she barely kept herself from keeling over.

"Better yet, Flynn's casting director came on board this week. Flynn didn't say specifically, but I got the impression that if my agent calls him, he'd connect her with casting. Maybe even give me a recommendation. I'm not sure though. He was hard to read." She cocked her head at Vicky, her gaze narrowed and speculative. "That's what you do for a living, isn't it? Read people? Maybe you could talk to him. Get a feel for what he's really thinking."

"Sure." Vicky would have said anything at that point to keep Ronnie there. "Will he be here tonight?"

"Ye-es." Ronnie's scorn wasn't well hidden. "As you said, everyone who's anyone is here tonight. Flynn is more than 'anyone.' He's an executive producer."

"Right." As if dozens of brilliant communications scientists and community leaders were dust beneath the feet of an executive producer. Vicky prevented her eyes from rolling by shifting them over Ronnie's shoulder.

Just as Zan Sinclair strode into the room.

Her heart jumped into her throat. On television, in his beautifully cut suits, he was handsome and assured. In person, she found him virile and commanding.

But here, now, in his black-and-white tux with his black head above everyone around him except for Dr. Winters, he dominated the room and stole her breath. Her heart started pounding again, and her hands slicked up. She rubbed them against her dress, leaving streaks.

Damn it, no. Her nerves were ruining her dress, and her misguided heart would ruin Ronnie's evening. She was Ronnie's wingman and no more.

Behind Zan were Nathaniel Winters and the blond Santa-Claus form of executive producer Flynn Roberts, followed by a stout, silver-haired man in a long-tailed jacket and burgundy bow tie whom she recognized as Dr. Josiah Johnson, the convention's primary organizer.

Vicky's eyes switched back to Zan as if magically compelled.

Ronnie's wingman.

Except apparently, incredibly, he'd really come here to meet *her*.

No, no. She couldn't do that to Ronnie—despite Ronnie having done it to her more than once. Maybe *because* Ronnie had done it to her; she knew the pain that came from it.

And while it was extremely unlikely she and Zan Sinclair could ever have a relationship, if they did, she wanted it to start cleanly. Which meant not hurting her sister.

Surprisingly, Zan also wanted any budding relationship between them to start cleanly, going so far as to take pains to meet her through her sister. Even though it hadn't worked, his heart was in the right place.

Almost as if he knew the hurt potential too.

Had he had his own Ronnie, unintentionally digging the blade deep? Her heart went out to him.

Immediately, she chastised herself. Pain like hers, right. Was she trying to bring him down to her level?

She briefly palmed her forehead. Much more of this and she could be the actress, auditioning for the most tear-jerking soaps.

Her job was simple. Be here for Ronnie. Avoid pictures like yesterday's. And try not to be so clumsy in front of Sinclair.

She glanced his way. That wouldn't be easy with him looking so handsome in his tux, especially if he looked at her like the newspaper photo, all that burning desire directed at *her*.... The memory rushed through her, exploding into a liquid need in her pelvis and thighs, so potent her legs trembled. She shuffled her feet, trying to ease her leg muscles.

And tripped.

She barely caught herself. Be here for Ronnie, avoid the press? Simple compared to the goal of not making an ass of herself. *Good luck with that one.*

Across the crowded ballroom, Zan's dark head lifted. As if he sensed something.

As if he sensed *her.*

His gaze traveled like a sword, cutting through the crowd.

Their eyes met.

Vicky's breath froze in her chest. He was so damned beautiful. So damned smart and strong.

So damned impossible, at least for someone like her. She looked away.

Couldn't help herself from looking back almost immediately.

He was coming for her.

CHAPTER EIGHT

Vicky blinked. Zan was plowing straight through the dazzling crowd as if he were a battle cruiser.

Her lips parted. Her heart started pounding. Her stomach fluttered with migrating butterflies, and her nerves sang chaotic technopop. The closer he got, the more her skin tingled, the hairs rising on her arms and nape, as if electricity charged her body—or as if her very hair and skin were reaching out for him.

Ronnie, with a quick couple steps, intercepted him. "Alex, there you are, naughty boy. You could have invited us to drinks in the greenroom with you and Flynn and the rest."

"Ronnie." Zan slowed. His eyes, over Ronnie's head, were locked on Vicky.

Desire burned in their black depths.

Vicky swallowed hard.

"Silly boy. I'm down here." Ronnie playfully touched his arm.

A simple sway moved him past her. He came straight to Vicky and took her hands.

Vicky couldn't meet his brilliant eyes. She stared at the floor and shook her head. She whispered, "This isn't right. You're supposed to be with Ronnie."

"I know. I will. I just had to...just wanted to say hi." He skimmed his fingertips over her cheek.

His fingers were blazing hot. She closed her eyes as an involuntary shiver of pleasure shimmered through her. "Hi." Her voice was hoarse.

"Are we done greeting each other?" Acid dripped in Ronnie's tone.

Vicky cracked her eyes to see her sister standing beside them, fists on hips, one eyebrow arched high.

Zan gave her hand a final squeeze before turning gracefully to Ronnie. "Can I get you some refreshment?" His glance back at Vicky made it plain he meant to get them both drinks. "You two can mingle while you wait. Or if you prefer, you can meet Nate and me at the head table."

"You'll get *me* refreshment?" The eyebrow stayed arched. "What about Vicky?"

"Nate will get your sister her drink," he corrected smoothly. "Here he comes now."

Nate Winters strode up. "Ladies." He turned to Zan. "Josiah said dinner will start in fifteen minutes. After the call to order, he'll want you to say a few brief words. Give us a toast to kick things off."

Ronnie butted between the two men. "Alex promised to get me a drink first. And *you* should get something for Vicky."

"Grow up," Nate said shortly, his eyes sparking at Ronnie before he spun off.

"Hey." Ronnie glared at Nate's broad back. "I'm the wronged party here."

But Zan caught Vicky's gaze over her sister's head, and there was a warmth to his eyes, and the slight crinkle of humor. Vicky knew why. She'd heard it too—Ronnie's tone was annoyed, but there wasn't any pain in it. Her ego was pricked, not her heart. Which relieved Vicky to no end.

And opened the door to *maybe*, sometime. A clean start.

Zan left for the bar. Vicky watched him go.

"Get your eyes off his ass and come with me." Ronnie grabbed Vicky's wrist and dragged her in the other direction. "I'll talk to Flynn Roberts while you do your communications woo-woo on him."

"It's not woo-woo." Vicky stumbled along behind, her gaze flicking back to Zan. "And how do you know where to find Mr. Roberts?"

"He came in with Alex and the rest. I've been tracking him."

Of course she had. Keeping track of her career while Vicky only had eyes for Zan, confirming her sister's priorities—a relief in one sense, but scaring Vicky with the strength of her own fascination.

"There he is. Now act surprised."

"Act like we're not stalking him?" Vicky grimaced; she hadn't meant to get snippy. Zan's heated touch, his hot interest, had thrown her. "Sorry."

"Make it up to me by reading Flynn. Remember— surprised." Ronnie edged toward Flynn Roberts, who was walking away from one of the bars, absently stirring a short glass of amber liquid. "Mr. Roberts! Fancy meeting you here."

His eyes lifted. "Hello, Dr. Brooks. Ms. Rivers, call me Flynn, remember?"

Ronnie's face lit up like a light bulb. "Flynn. I was thinking about what you said yesterday, how hard it is to cast a pilot when you barely have a handle on the characters..."

Vicky knew she was supposed to be reading Flynn, but she couldn't help watching her sister with awe. As a supermodel, Ronnie knew how to work the crowd, but she was a goddess working a single person.

In fact, ten minutes later, when the call to find their seats came—a barely heard announcement by stout organizer Josiah Johnson from the head table—Ronnie was still talking.

"Excuse me," Vicky said. "Shouldn't we go sit? We're supposed to meet Dr. Sinclair and Dr. Winters in front." She'd managed to watch Flynn Roberts for Ronnie...in between keeping track of Zan. Ten minutes ago, he and Nate had easily cut through the lines at a bar and gotten two drinks each, but they'd been delayed returning with those drinks, stopping to chat with seemingly every group or person on the way.

"Dinner won't actually start for another ten or more minutes. We have time." Ronnie turned back to Flynn, coaxing playfully, "So, casting your pilot episode, which character would you see me as?"

"Hmm." The rotund little man rubbed his beard thoughtfully.

Ronnie flicked eyes to Vicky, then Flynn, then her gaze narrowed dangerously at Vicky. Vicky sighed but dutifully cranked up her "woo-woo" communications skills.

And to her shock, she saw Flynn was *faking it.*

Oh, he was listening to Ronnie's subtle and not-so-subtle flattery and acting terribly receptive, but underneath—he'd already made up his mind to recommend her to casting.

How had that happened? He hadn't met Ronnie before lunch. Had he seen her in one of her limited roles? Wanted her on the strength of her range as Dead Body #1? Unless...Flynn was Zan's producer. Could Zan have not just piqued Flynn's interest in Ronnie but engineered Flynn's decision?

She shuddered. If so, Alexander Sinclair was more powerful and well connected than she'd known.

"Ladies and gentlemen." Zan's voice rang strongly over the PA, confirming her gut impression. "If you would please find your seats, dinner is about to begin."

The crowd immediately started shuffling toward the center of the room, filtering through the hundred tables to find a thousand seats.

"And now I must leave you lovely ladies." Flynn pressed Ronnie's hands with his and leaned in for the two-cheek buss Vicky was seeing was the norm for this set.

Ronnie waved brightly until he turned away. Then she grabbed Vicky's hand and towed her toward the head table. "Damn, I'm parched. I hope the boys got us our drinks. I could use one. What did you see?"

"Um, well, I think he's interested." Vicky wasn't sure how much she should reveal to Ronnie. It was mostly assumption on her part—true, made on the basis of experience and education, but there was still the smallest chance she was wrong. If she told Ronnie she was as good as in and then nothing happened, Ronnie would be disappointed. "I think he's seriously considering presenting your information to casting for this pilot."

"Really?" The girlish sparkle in Ronnie's eyes told Vicky she'd done the right thing. Ronnie's hopes were truly engaged with this. Better to be vague than sorry.

They reached the dais. Nathaniel Winters was waiting for them at the bottom of a set of portable stairs. "Ladies." He offered his hand to Ronnie. "Ms. Rivers, you're right next to the podium."

"The seat of honor?" With a smug smile, Ronnie gathered her skirt with one hand, put the other in Nate's, and gracefully swayed up the three steps. At the top, he released her hand, repositioned himself, and, while Zan seated Ronnie, held his hand out to Vicky.

Okay. The goal wasn't to look as good as the accomplished Ronnie Rivers. The goal was not to fall on her butt and embarrass herself. She grabbed a handful of skirt, put her other hand in Nate's, sucked in a breath for courage, and set her foot on the first step.

His strength buttressed her. Amazingly, she didn't trip, fall, or even stumble. She raised herself up with the aid of Nate's firm grip and put her foot on the next step, then the next...and then she was on the dais, miraculously without incident.

She felt like cheering.

"You're sitting there." Nate pointed to the seat three from the podium.

Heavens, so near the center. She took another deep breath and started toward it.

And saw Zan turn toward her, a glass of white wine dwarfed by his hand. He moved with an animal grace that made her belly throb. He smiled. The white teeth, the gleam in his dark eyes, arrowed straight to her heart. "Your wine." He held out the glass.

She swallowed hard, her whole body prickling with moisture, swelling with it. "Thanks." Her tone was embarrassingly breathy. She raised her hand for the glass, couldn't quite reach it, and took a step toward him.

And tripped.

Her stomach plummeted...and then he was there, catching her in one strong arm before she'd even known she was doing a header.

He gathered her to him, pressed her along his body. His heat seared her through her thin gown.

She tilted her face up to apologize. His black eyes were burning down at her. She locked gazes helplessly with him and licked her lips. His gaze went molten.

"Zan?" Nate wedged himself between them and the table. He nodded almost imperceptibly at the crowded room over his shoulder.

He'd positioned himself in front of them, shielding them from a thousand people who might get the wrong idea. Who might take a picture and share that wrong idea with a million more.

Her cheeks burned. She'd had three goals, and she'd tanked two. Straightening, she pushed away from Zan's strong body.

He hesitated letting her go, almost as if he were reluctant to do it.

Behind him, Ronnie cleared her throat. "What's going on here?"

Vicky tried to step back...and nearly fell off the platform again. Only Zan's quick reflexes saved her.

Then Ronnie was shoving them apart. Vicky fell against Nate Winters so hard he grunted with the impact.

"Alex." Ronnie's tone was tight, and her eyes spat twin forks of lightning. "You sit next to the podium. I'll sit where you were going to, in seat two. Nate, you sit next to me in seat three. And Vicky"—she took the glass from Zan's hand and plunked it in place setting four—"will sit here. Where you can't get into any more *trouble.*"

* * *

Zan's gaze was drawn down the table to Vicky for the fiftieth time that night. Her pretty pink lips slid over her fork just as he'd like them to slide over *him....* It was driving him crazy. It was just as well Ronnie had foiled his original seating plan. If he'd sat next to Vicky as he wanted, he wouldn't have been able to keep his hands off her.

He wasn't sure he could keep them off her even now.

No, he had to behave. In the interest of clean beginnings, before he could pursue Vicky, Ronnie's misconceptions needed to be settled. While keeping the picture hounds off his tail.

And he needed to deal with whatever Vicky meant when she said that he and she were "worlds apart."

Her tongue darted out to claim a last bit of sauce on her fork. His whole body coiled so tightly his muscles twitched with the need to throw her to the dais and pound himself into her.

Okay, the "worlds apart" wasn't all he could think of.

In fact, it was hard to think of anything at all, because he wanted her. Wanted to kiss her so badly he trembled with it. Wanted to take her up to his suite and drag her into the bedroom and throw her on the bed....

He shuddered. Grabbed his ice water and drank the entire glass in two gulps. God. For a man who prided himself on being free of communications-clouding emotion, he was feeling a helluva lot right now.

Somewhere in that interminably long meal punctuated by interminably long speeches—including his own—he rationalized his burning desire. He needed to know if they were compatible physically. Why hurt her by pursuing her only to break it off if they weren't compatible?

Yes. He not only wanted to touch her, he *needed* to touch her. Kiss her. And it had to happen before the end of the convention.

Immediately, he felt better. Clearer-headed. More in control.

And now that he knew it needed to be done, why put it off? The sooner the better. In fact, tonight.

As soon as dinner was over, he'd get her alone and kiss her.

Tonight. He felt even better at that thought. And it left plenty of time before the end of the conference to gently break it to Ronnie that he wasn't interested in her, so that he could have that clean beginning with Vicky.

Perfect.

Nate stood and made yet another toast. Zan raised his glass, practiced smile on his lips, and pretended to listen. When Nate finished by clinking glasses with Vicky, Zan automatically turned to touch his to Ronnie's.

The blonde was watching him *very* closely, a cutting intelligence in her eyes.

It woke him from his lustful haze, alerted him to the danger he was in. He smothered the lust, changed it out for a toothy grin, and touched his glass to hers.

As he sipped, Ronnie's fingers tiptoed into his lap.

Shock propelled him to intercept her before he was even truly aware what she was doing. He grabbed her hand, stopping her exploration.

She gave him a half-smile and a shrug, as if to say *no harm*. Then she laced her fingers with his and wouldn't let go.

And he began to see the primary problem wouldn't be getting Vicky alone but getting free of her sister.

As he ate, Zan kept his eyes open for an opportunity. As soon as the entrees were served to the back of the room—and Vicky hadn't eaten much of hers—she disappeared from the dais.

Zan immediately rose to follow her.

Or rather, half-rose, because Ronnie tightened her hold on his hand and wouldn't let go. He tried to gently peel her off. Finger by finger, he gained his freedom. One finger to go…and just as he peeled loose, she demanded he get her another drink.

After which she cast a significant glance at the assembled diners.

He didn't have to be a communications expert to understand that glance. If he left now, everyone would see it and wonder why he was taking off in the middle of dinner and where he was going.

So, while his blood boiled to follow Vicky, he went to the nearest bar instead and got Ronnie a drink. Returning to the table was like wading through hip-high glue. He set the wine gently, so very gently, in front of her, because he wanted to slam it down in frustration. He'd lost his best chance to follow Vicky.

Fingers clenching, he sat, holding himself as tight and straight as a steel bar in his chair. Dessert was served. He craned for a glimpse of Vicky returning so often his neck and back began to ache from the strain.

Through what would normally have been a delightful key lime pie, his chafing grew into desperation as Ronnie clung to him harder and harder. Which surprised him, actually; she'd never been needy before, not even when he'd been dating her. He turned his head to look at her, really look. She smiled brightly into his eyes and grafted herself to his arm.

He blinked in surprise. She had something riding on him, something important. If he left her right now, it would truly hurt her somehow—not her feelings, but something.

And while he was growing closer and closer to the point where he didn't give a damn, Vicky cared about her sister. He found himself strangely reluctant to disappoint Vicky.

So he waited until his key lime pie was crumbs on his plate. Until dessert was served to the last tables. Until the coffee was cool in his cup.

Until he could stand it no longer.

Surreptitiously, he waved Flynn up to the table.

Flynn took his time, sauntering over like a smug Santa Claus—he knew what Zan was up to. Zan hadn't said anything about Vicky to the producer, so his friend Nate—his soon-to-be-vasectomied friend Nate—must have talked.

Flynn took his time, and Zan chafed, wishing for once he wasn't a communications wonk understanding every nonverbal behavioral nuance. Flynn's sauntering said he'd help Zan. And that darn smirk said Flynn was going to exact a few pounds of flesh for his assistance.

And Zan...didn't care. His blood boiled to pursue Vicky. Caution had flown out the window on wings of need. The instant Flynn mounted the dais, Zan pried himself loose from Ronnie without any subtlety whatsoever, rose, and shoved Flynn into his own chair.

But as he strode down the stairs, Ronnie called after him. "Alex, be a dear and get me another drink."

He spun, burning with anger. Damn, how desperate was she, to pull that again? Didn't matter. He was done playing her games. He motioned to Nate, still on the dais. Nate was deep in conversation with the silver-haired, sophisticated woman, socialite and professor emeritus Leda Loper, who'd moved into Vicky's chair to chat with him.

Nate didn't hear him.

Frustrated beyond sanity, Zan plucked up a napkin from a passing waiter distributing champagne, dunked it into some bubbly, twisted it into a ball, and winged it at Nate's head.

The napkin ball missed Nate but landed in his glass of water, splashing his hand. Nate raised an annoyed eyebrow at Zan. What the hell; it got his attention.

Zan used a combination of hand signals and simple desperation to convey what he needed. Nate's smile was half-exasperation, half-sympathy.

But he got up and headed for the bar.

Great. Now for a fast getaway. Zan spun for the bank of ballroom doors.

As he strode away, he made the mistake of glancing back.

Ronnie was coming off the dais, steaming straight for him.

Zan was an adult male of exceptional size. He'd trained in martial arts, weapons fighting, and other disciplines in the Marines. He was not afraid of *anyone*.

Yet he saw Ronnie chasing him and scooted out of there like his short hairs were on fire. He banged through one of the ballroom doors practically running.

CHAPTER NINE

Halfway down the hallway, Zan slowed. What was he doing? He didn't owe Ronnie anything. He'd made no commitments. He didn't have to flee her. He glanced behind him.

A door slammed open. Ronnie stood in the doorway like a golden avenging angel.

He spun and kicked into a lope.

He was exquisitely aware of how ridiculously he was behaving. He certainly hoped no paparazzi caught him running down the hallway like a scared kid. Maybe he could say he was training for his show. Or a feature film. Or the Zombie Apocalypse. Ronnie did feel like a brain-eating zombie shambling inexorably behind him.

At least that was his excuse why, despite being in excellent shape, he was panting and out of breath by the time he reached the cross corridor.

He zipped around the corner to his right. He found himself in a shorter hallway. Doors were spaced every twenty feet or so—the session rooms. He slowed to a walk and caught his breath.

"Alex? Alex, where are you going?" Always high, Ronnie's voice grated on Zan's nerves like shards of glass. She was close and coming fast.

Hide, *now*. He zipped into the first doorway and pressed himself flat.

The doorways were shallow, no more than six inches deep. Half his chest jutted out and probably his feet and the tip of his nose as well.

Damn. He spun and pulled on the door. It didn't budge. He tugged harder but it was locked. Double damn.

He raced across the hallway. Tried that door.

Locked too. He dug both hands into his hair.

"Alex? Where are you? What are you doing?"

He jerked around so fast he lost hair. He desperately scanned the hallway for a hiding place, any hiding place.

Ronnie's heels thudded ever nearer on the carpet-covered concrete, about to round the corner.

Farther down the corridor, a single white linen-covered table beckoned like a draped angel.

He took two running steps and dove under it.

"*Alex*? Where the hell is that man?"

The tablecloth fluttered down behind him. It was full-length, brushing the floor. On all fours, he dropped his head to peer under it. He saw nothing. He dared to lift a tiny peephole. Ronnie was wheeling around the corner. He dropped the cloth as if it'd burned him.

"Alex, come on. Enough." Her voice was barely muffled by the tablecloth. "Come out, come out, wherever you are."

He peeked again. Her gold pumps flashed by, red and white crystals catching the light and sending a glint directly into his brain. It cut his skull like a migraine.

"This is no longer funny, Alex." Her volume tapered as she continued down the hallway.

He lifted the tablecloth again and didn't see her. He stuck his head out and peered around.

She was standing farther down the corridor with her back to him, tapping one foot.

He took a chance. Crept out. And dashed down the hallway the way he'd come.

He'd barely reached the cross corridor when he heard her shriek, "Alex!"

Busted. He sprinted to his right, away from the ballroom.

The corridor stretched out in front of him like an airport runway. The few doorways were shallow. The restrooms were far, far in the distance. No convenient refreshment tables stood nearby to hide under.

Then he saw the sign "Cry Room." He dove for it and wrenched the handle.

It was unlocked.

He threw the door open, rushed into the semi-dark room, and slammed the door shut behind him.

* * *

Vicky had come to the Cry Room to be alone with her churning thoughts. She'd crushed afar on Dr. Alexander Sinclair for so long. Ten years ago, long before *Secrets* had made him a household name, long before he'd earned his billions, she'd bought his first book on a whim. His energetic style and fresh ideas had immediately enthralled her. Then five years ago, he'd made his first appearance on a public television talk show, and she was completely hooked.

It seemed pure fantasy that he returned her interest. A dream come true. Well, come true but for the complication of her sister. And his wealth and position. And half a continent between them.

A dream. Right. An impossible dream.

She took a deep breath. Time to face reality. Time to put the attractive but impossible dream out of her head. She let the breath out, took another.

The door flew open and slammed shut. She turned. The breath stuck in her lungs.

Zan Sinclair stood there. Tall. Elegant. Dark. So handsome she wanted to nibble every stark plane.

She opened her mouth to say something, anything.

No words came out.

"Vicky. Oh, God."

Then he was sweeping down on her and pulling her into an embrace as tight as her throat, and no words were needed.

His fingers threaded through her hair. "I can't stand it." His voice was hoarse. "The need, every time I'm near you, to do this." He secured her head at the nape, tilted her face up—and kissed her.

Her lips parted on a gasp of surprise, drawing in a taste of lime and whiskey. He began to caress his mouth over hers, his lips warm. Desire stirred in her belly. Her eyelids fluttered closed, and she whimpered softly.

At the sound, he groaned. He brushed his tongue along the seam of her lips, urging her to open more fully to him. Her lips throbbed to do as he asked— and so did she. She slid her palms onto his firm chest and leaned up, her mouth opening to him in invitation.

His tongue swept in, gently conquering. Fulfilling her deepest desires, her deepest needs, stirring her belly, igniting liquid fire in her veins. The lava desire was beyond anything she'd ever experienced. *He* was more than she'd ever experienced, and far more than she'd dreamed. She pressed against him and squirmed, not to arouse him, but because her nipples and very skin cells were screaming with need. Her inexperience made her awkward.

It didn't matter. He responded to her artless embrace by crushing her to his chest and kissing her with fury and fire and insatiable hunger.

She kissed him back with equal passion.

"*What is going on here?*"

Under Vicky's palms, Zan stiffened. He lifted his head, a low growl rumbling in his chest.

Abruptly, it cut off.

93

She fought her way up through her feverish haze to identify the voice.

"What are you doing?" The shriek came from the door. "What the hell do you think you're doing?"

The shriek was Ronnie's.

* * *

The next morning, Zan's heart thudded hollowly in his chest as he loaded Ronnie's luggage in the chauffeured black Lincoln Town Car. Ronnie had texted him, pointedly telling him he was giving her a ride to the airport. Nearby, on the sidewalk, Vicky chafed her arms and examined dust, in another world for all the attention she paid him.

When he'd first seen Vicky here too, he'd been relieved and grateful, thinking Ronnie had arranged it so they could talk things out. Ronnie had arranged it, but not to talk.

He kept glancing at Vicky, hoping to meet her eye. Hoping to have the conversation they hadn't been able to have since Ronnie had torn them apart, even if it was only unspoken.

Hoping to tell Vicky that he wanted, so very much, to see her again.

But Ronnie was standing there, tapping her toe, slicing everyone with cutting glares, him and her sister both.

Probably why Vicky, the tips of her ears very red, was staring at the sidewalk.

It wasn't fair at all. Why should she pay the penalty of her sister's wrath because *he* had lost control? He tried again to tell Ronnie that. "Ronnie, it was *my* fault, not Vic—"

"Darling Alex. Do you think I care?" Her tone was all sugar, like a poisoned soft drink. The venomous speed with which she cut him off shouted her true feelings. "Well, I don't. I don't care one bit." The B in bit was explosive, the T snapped off as she'd probably like to do to his head.

He sighed. This was a lose-lose situation and why clean starts were so important. He'd screwed that royally.

The awkward, painful silence seemed to stretch forever, but only a few moments went by as he and the limo driver loaded the luggage. The driver shut the trunk with a click. As if it was a cue, Ronnie dropped her tightly crossed arms and advanced on her sister.

Vicky finally looked up. The misery on her face tugged at Zan's heart. He took one step toward her.

As if Ronnie sensed him moving, she glared at him over her shoulder. "Alex. Why don't you wait in the car while I say goodbye to my sister?" The words were honey-frosted anger.

He ignored her. His gaze had finally meshed with Vicky's. And hers...damn, her eyes were pleading with him not to make this any more difficult than it was. He faltered. He opened his palms to her, knowing his need, his pain, was on his face. *Are you sure?*

She nodded, flushed red, and glanced away. Nodded again, tiny, almost to herself.

He balled his fists. What the hell did that second nod mean? Did she want him but was trying to convince herself he should stay away?

Or was that final peal of certainty a sign she never wanted to see him again?

His fingers clenched, and he knew from the ache starting in his head that he was grinding his teeth. He, Alexander Sinclair, communications expert, couldn't read that nod, and it was driving him crazy.

He spun away. Whatever the underlying meaning, she wanted him to leave her alone. To go without saying the words in his suddenly too-full heart. He'd honor that.

He strode abruptly back to the limo. The driver stood at attention by the open back door. Zan grabbed the roof and propelled himself inside. He crossed his arms and felt furiously sorry for himself in the darkened limo for exactly two seconds.

Then he slid to the edge of the seat, placed one foot on the pavement, and gazed out at Vicky, willing her to look at him one last time. Needing her to be as reluctant to leave him as he was to leave her.

Hoping she cared for him, just a little.

"Sister dearest." Ronnie's red and crystal earrings flashed in the sun as she gave Vicky a double air-kiss. "Goodbye. I'd like to say it's been fun."

Vicky's return "goodbye" was a tiny, forlorn sound.

Zan's heart broke. He hoped she wasn't also saying it to him and meaning forever.

"Goodbye," he echoed from within the limo.

Ronnie turned from Vicky and clipped irritated heels along the sidewalk to the limo. "We're going." She shoved in with more force than necessary.

Zan slid to the other side of the car, out of her blast radius, as the driver clicked the door shut behind her.

She sat in stony silence as the limo pulled away from the curb.

In a nightmare replay of the first time he'd glimpsed Vicky at LAX, Zan peeked past Ronnie's stony profile for a last glimpse of Vicky. He saw her flash by the side window and turned in his seat, watching until he couldn't see her anymore. He wondered if he would ever see her again.

* * *

Vicky stood like a stone statue, watching the limo drive away. As it disappeared around a curve, it felt like her heart was disappearing with it.

She'd felt free to crush on Zan Sinclair from afar because she thought she'd never meet him. She'd never have to hear him tell her how impossible they were. Never have her heart broken.

Then she'd met him for real, and shockingly, he'd told her just the opposite. He was interested in her.

That hungry kiss last night had confirmed it.

But it had told her something else, something just as important.

She was attracted to him too. She was attracted to, not just the image of Sinclair on her television, but the man himself.

Her crush wasn't pure fantasy. She was definitely physically attracted to the real Zan Sinclair. And the real Zan Sinclair was definitely physically attracted to her.

Which didn't say anything about their underlying emotions. But she knew she felt *something* for him. The question was, were they the kind of feelings that could last?

She nearly smacked herself on the head. Lasting feelings, like her and Zan Sinclair and happily ever after—after just four days? Back to fantasy, big-time.

She broke out of her stupid-sculpture trance, grabbed the handle of her suitcase, and left the curb to trundle back inside the hotel, leaving her insane hopes behind her like so much rubbish.

The hotel was blissfully cool and, compared to the bustle of the convention in full swing yesterday, only buzzed with people packing up detritus to go home.

It was all so impossible. Even if *her* feelings were the kind that could last, a real relationship took two people. His feelings were probably very temporary. Good heavens, in a few weeks, he might not even remember her. Just because he'd imprinted her for life didn't mean she'd had the same long-lasting effect on him. Just because she'd thought his eyes were filled with longing for her didn't mean a thing, no matter how much she wanted it to.

In the parking garage, she loaded her suitcase into the trunk of her very-definitely-not-a-limo Suzuki, wishing she were snuggled up in the dark backseat of his limo with him instead....

So much for leaving her feelings curbside.

She paid for her parking and started home. She had to stop thinking about him. He'd probably put her from his mind already; she needed to do the same. Her goodbye had come from the depths of her heart, but his was no doubt the high school graduation kind—tearful promises to get together, meaning it with the best of intentions, but never quite doing it.

She did not fit in his world.

Except there were times...times she'd seen glimpses. Ways he'd acted, and reacted, that told her there was more to Zan Sinclair than the handsome, untouchable perfection he projected on his show. More than the billionaire playboy who had a fresh girlfriend every few weeks.

Little things that hinted she and Zan might be more alike than they seemed.

She sighed as she merged onto I-70 headed east. Right. And while all that might be true, it was also true that he was an extremely busy man. Even if he remembered her, when would he find time to call her, much less get together? Besides, the half a country between them included a few tiny things called mountains.

Then there was still the little matter of clean beginnings. Where did Ronnie's feelings and needs come in all this?

And why was Ronnie still interested in Zan?

Vicky's thoughts detoured for a moment. It *was* curious. As girls, Ronnie had innocently stolen a number of Vicky's boyfriends because she got bored. Once stolen, bored Ronnie quickly moved on, never hanging on to any one boyfriend for long—a couple months at most.

Ronnie had had Zan last year. Past behavior said Ronnie should be over him by now.

So why was she hanging on?

Were her sister's feelings perhaps real? Zan was fascinating, rich, and successful—everything Ronnie could want.

But there was the small matter of his not wanting Ronnie in return. Ronnie had never wasted time on a boy who didn't want her; she had too many interested in her for her to bother with one who wasn't. Had that changed?

Or was it simply that Ronnie had gotten mad at Vicky for stealing what she considered hers, and was taking revenge? Ronnie could nurse anger into a mad that would last for years.

Vicky sighed. Talk about futile. Whatever the cause, Ronnie was definitely angry. It didn't matter why. If Vicky ever wanted to enjoy her sister's company again, she'd better call to apologize. Ronnie hadn't been receptive last night or this morning, but surely without Vicky there to exacerbate things, Ronnie would thaw some. Timing, with her sister's moods, was everything.

Vicky decided to call the moment she got home. Hopefully Ronnie would be open to an apology.

* * *

Vicky unlocked her apartment door, kicked it open, dropped her suitcase in the entryway, dumped her purse on the first available surface, and dug out her cell phone.

But when she called Ronnie to apologize, it went to voice mail.

Darn it. Vicky slammed her door shut and threw the bolt harder than necessary. That was bad. Had Ronnie already worked herself into a state? Was she refusing to answer?

She called back. Same thing. She clicked End with a curse—and without leaving a voice mail. If Ronnie was in a mood, a message would only make things worse.

She picked up her suitcase and wheeled it into her bedroom. Then she dropped the suitcase, flopped onto her bed, and tried calling again. She really wanted to get this over with.

Same thing. She covered her eyes with her hand and thought about crying, or getting very drunk.

Then she realized the phone had gone *directly* to voice mail, without ringing. As if it was shut off.

Could Ronnie still be in the air? Vicky had made the run from Kansas City to St. Louis in less than three and a half hours. Even a nonstop flight had to go over a big swatch of mountains.

Vicky called back and, this time, left a message. Then she got up off the bed and kept herself busy unpacking. Tried to keep her mind off what was coming.

She unfolded the green dress.

It was going to be hard to apologize to her sister for something she didn't really regret.

A deep sigh inflated her chest. She exhaled, and it left her flatter than before. Her gorgeous Gala dress, paid for by Zan Sinclair. She held its hanger in one hand, the silky fabric of the sleek skirt in the other, and blinked damp eyes.

The dress made her think of who she might have been, had she grown up a different way. If her sister had not been the impossibly beautiful one, sealing Vicky into the role of the smart one.

She clutched the lovely dress to her. If only she were smart and pretty both, a woman who could grace this rich dress and who, in it, could walk proudly on Zan's arm into the loftiest realms of high society.

She released her tight hold on the material and molded it against her body. For a moment, she let the dream take her—wearing the dress in Zan's strong arms. She danced a few steps around her bedroom.

And promptly hit her leg against the corner of the bed, tripped, and took a header.

She managed to fall without mangling the dress too badly. The knee she scraped seemed almost an afterthought, though one that stung. Scrambling to her feet, she dropped the dress on her bed and blinked at it again. The fabric shimmered in her eyes. Hot liquid trickled down one cheek.

She sighed deeply, dashed the tear away, went to her closet, and pushed the hangers until she'd exposed the back of the closet. There she hung the dress, and her dreams, where she couldn't be reminded of them.

The phone rang, Ronnie's ringtone. Vicky shut the closet door, took a cleansing breath, and prepared to deal with her sister.

CHAPTER TEN

"Thanks for calling," Vicky said.

"What do you want?" Ronnie's clipped tone said she wasn't going to let Vicky off easily.

"I just called to...well, I wanted to apologize for what happened at CommuniCon. I was supposed to be your wingman, and I...I let my emotions overcome my better judgment. I'm so very sorry. I hope you'll forgive me."

There was a moment's silence. Vicky held her breath. Then Ronnie sighed. "No, it's understandable."

Vicky's breath eased out. Thank goodness her sister didn't often hold grudges.

Then she added, "He *is* pretty damned sexy. You were just curious."

Vicky's mouth dropped open. From her perspective, it had been more, much more, than her simply being "curious" about Zan. But she managed to swallow a tart retort and only said, "It's not like anything could come of it. You said it yourself. You and Winters and Sinclair are in California, and I'm here in Missouri. No chance of anything happening."

"No chance." Ronnie's tone brightened at that. "Yes. A relationship is completely out of the question. Impossible. You really don't have a chance with either of them."

No chance with Zan.

Hearing Ronnie state it so baldly stabbed Vicky with icicles. She needed to change the subject immediately. She opened her mouth but nothing came out.

"Especially not with Alex," Ronnie went on. "You know, at first I was worried. He was distracted on the flight back, and I thought maybe he was thinking about you and the convention. But then he took out his phone and started working. He wouldn't do that if he was pining over you, would he?"

Ronnie's words stabbed into an already hurting wound. Vicky had to say something, *anything,* to stop Ronnie, but she had trouble swallowing past the big lump of misery in her throat.

"In LA, he shared another limo with me. And on the way to my apartment, he told me he wanted us to stay in touch. He wouldn't have done that if he wanted a fling with my older sister."

Vicky flinched. Ronnie wasn't calculating enough to deliberately choose words to wound, but *fling* and *older* put Vicky in her place like a thousand snubs. She was no beautiful, brilliant young thing to capture a powerful, rich man's attention, much less his love.

"Yes," she finally choked out. "You're right, I'm sure." She swallowed hard. "So. Are we good?"

"We're good." Ronnie sounded chipper as always.

Vicky ended the call, glad she'd made up with her sister.

But in her chest, her heart and her hopes had shriveled.

* * *

Zan Sinclair, while deployed as a Marine, had cleared buildings of insurgents, motored down the middle of IED-infested roads, and tackled any number of highly dangerous jobs. But now he walked a tightrope thinner and more treacherous than anything he'd ever attempted before.

He was trying to stay on friendly terms with a woman who wanted him while pursuing her sister.

It was enough to make him question his sanity.

But the combination of his heart prodding him and his libido shouting at him meant backing off wasn't an option.

He didn't use his office at the studio very often, but for this, he needed privacy. Sitting at his desk, he set his tablet computer on the surface, synced it with his PA's, then checked his calendar to figure out when he could visit Vicky. He was looking for a hole of a couple days, *without* shifting or canceling appointments. Significant changes could tip off the media, and it would certainly tip off Ronnie, who'd gotten quite chummy with his PA's assistant. And if Ronnie got wind of his visiting Vicky, she'd have no qualms about crashing St. Louis, and things would be worse than before.

His gaze flicked over the stuffed squares that masqueraded as weekdays and weekends. Damn. His schedule was packed, as usual. Scripts due, assessment meetings with his research graduates, and a variety of regular production tasks crowded his days and social necessities blocked out his nights, not to mention all the catching up he needed to do because of the convention.

Okay, maybe next week. He swept forward on the screen.

So many appointments greeted him that the week looked like a mass of black. He thumbed his aching temple.

But canceling would alert Ronnie...damn, he should have broken it off with her in no uncertain terms.

No, she was Vicky's sister, so he was trying to keep on her good side. That was why, on the flight back, though he'd kept a certain distance—hell, he'd told Ronnie he wasn't interested in her and wouldn't be dating her—he'd had to soften the blow by adding that they should stay in touch.

He hadn't missed the sparkle of speculation in Ronnie's eyes at that. He wasn't naive; Ronnie hadn't given up the idea that he was really subtly pursuing her.

He pinched the bridge of his nose. Her delusions were giving him a headache.

Worse, all this was distracting him from his true goal—convincing Vicky that he was interested in *her*. Which was going to take a bit more effort and tenacity than he'd first thought. *Worlds apart.* What the hell did that mean?

This whole situation made him feel stuffed in an emotional blender set on puree. He, Zan Sinclair, in trying to keep himself free of muddling emotion, had become totally muddled. It would have been funny if he could find his sense of humor in the blender's blades.

He wasn't thinking clearly, hadn't been since first breathing Vicky's soft scent. The only way he could think of to bring any clarity back to his life was to relieve his frustrated desire for her, which meant satisfying his deep craving for her.

Which meant visiting her.

His body tightened pleasantly at that. That kiss...it had fired him hotter and faster than any before. *Vicky* fired him hotter and faster. She was just so damned sweet. So soft. She fit so perfectly in his arms. Not to mention, he simply enjoyed being with her, talking to her, listening to her sweet voice....

Then Ronnie had stormed into that Cry Room, and Vicky had *pushed him away*. After which, she hadn't spoken more than three words to him, one of which was that heart-rending goodbye.

Hadn't she felt what he'd felt? How could she ignore him so totally if she had? He clutched the tablet until his knuckles turned white. It scared him. Could the kiss that had shaken him to his core have left her unaffected?

Had he misread the whole situation?

He'd done it before.

No. Consciously he released the casing. Even if he'd misread her response, *she* fit him perfectly. And he, in turn, would fit her, if he had to trim off his arms and legs to do it.

He scowled at his packed calendar. Swept back to this week. No hole jumped out at him. He barely had a free hour, much less days.

The buzz of the intercom made him nearly snarl. He picked up his office phone. "Yes, Mrs. Radlong?" He managed to make it civil—barely.

"You have your calendar open, sir?" His PA was a competent, middle-aged woman who'd been with him since he published his first book.

"Yes, why?"

"I need to add an appointment to it, and the week I want is locked."

"*Add* something?" This week was already a disaster.

Fuck that. Vicky was too important. He slashed three days at the end of the week. "No, Mrs. Radlong. You're not adding anything. In fact, cancel my appointments Friday through Sunday."

"Sir?"

"Get me plane, hotel, and car reservations for the same time period in St. Louis, Missouri. And *don't* tell your assistant."

"Oh. Yes, sir." There was a strange satisfaction in his PA's tone. Almost as if she knew why Zan had lost control and why he wanted her to cancel appointments. "Consider it done."

* * *

To Vicky's surprise, Ronnie called her just four days later, on Thursday.

In tears.

"He didn't want me," her sister wailed. "How could he not want me?"

"Ronnie, wait. Calm down." Vicky dropped the pen she was using to grade papers and pressed the phone harder to her ear, listening to every nuance. Who the hell didn't want her sister? Sinclair? Vicky would go after him with a meat cleaver. Sure, she wanted Zan for herself, but first, if he'd made her sister cry, she'd chop him into stew meat.

Because Ronnie didn't cry often, not real tears. Vicky hoped against hope that this wasn't belated fallout from CommuniCon—and that hotter-than-sin kiss. Which she hadn't been thinking of all week. Because she'd had to sleep sometime. Although even then, she'd dreamed about it...darn it. "Ronnie, take a deep breath. Then start from the beginning."

"Deep breath." Ronnie gave a choked little laugh. "That's the start of an acting exercise." And she burst into a fresh bout of tears.

"Acting? This is about acting?" Vicky felt a ridiculous amount of relief that *she* wasn't the cause of her sister's pain. Guilt muddied her relief. Who cared what the cause was? Ronnie was obviously hurting. "Deep breath, Ronnie, then tell me what happened."

A breath whooshed over the phone. "Thanks." Another. When Ronnie's voice came again, it was steadier. "Okay. Do you remember Flynn Roberts, the executive producer of Alex's show?"

"Blond Santa Claus, sure."

"Santa Claus. He felt like Santa to me." Ronnie's tone tightened as if she was throttling more tears. "He not only got the casting firm to call my agent, he got me an audition—for one of the main roles."

"But that's wonderful! Isn't it?"

"I thought so. I was in heaven. I'd finally gotten my big break. I thought I had it made." A hard swallow. "I'm nearly thirty. Doesn't mean much to you, but you're in a career where age isn't a thing."

"I understand. That's why trying to break into acting is so important to you."

"Trying, yes." She gave a watery hiccup. "I didn't get the role, Vicky. I got the break"—a sob—"but I didn't get the role."

"Oh, honey. There will be other roles."

"No, there won't!" Ronnie sobbed harder. "You don't understand. That was my big break."

"But Sinclair helped get you this break, right? Maybe he can get you another—"

"You don't understand!"

Vicky waited in shocked silence.

When Ronnie's voice came again, it was small. "My big break, and I...I screwed it up. *I* screwed it up. Even if there is a next time, what's to say I won't screw up that break too?"

"Next time you'll do better."

"I don't know *how* to do better," Ronnie wailed. "I don't understand acting, not like modeling. I *get* modeling. I know how to make the most of my looks, how to move my body to show product at its best. How to throw my personality out there, to draw the buyers in. But when I try the same thing with acting, it...it doesn't work."

Vicky listened hard. Frustration and anger colored Ronnie's voice—and underneath was a note of real fear. Her heart went out to her sister. If the things Ronnie had done before weren't working, without an idea how to fix it...she must feel helpless. "If there's anything I can do, just name it."

"Maybe you can tell me... How did you do it? You got great grades in school, went to college, and got a job right away. You have a career that will carry you to retirement. How did you manage all that?"

"Wow." Vicky had never realized how much she'd achieved. "How? Study. And lots of hard work."

"I'm working hard." Ronnie sniffed. "I'm pedaling my ass off. But it feels like I'm spinning my wheels. Or sometimes like I'm pedaling toward a cliff."

"That may be part of the problem. You have to set a good target first. A goal." Vicky pursed her lips. "One not remotely near a *cliff*."

A surprised laugh came over the phone. "Okay. I set a target? I want to be an actress."

"That's too broad, and you don't have control over many aspects of it. For a realistic goal, you have to pick something smaller, something where you can determine the outcome."

"But I want to be an actress. I don't have any other goals."

"Yes, but...look, you set a bunch of smaller goals that *move* toward the big one. Like, 'I'll take an acting class to improve my delivery.' Or 'I'll start singing lessons to work on my vocal quality.' Then you do it, over and over, until you get results."

"Phooey. That sounds hard."

"It can be. But it can also be fun. And it's nice to take control of your own life. Go after what you want." Vicky stared at the stack of student papers.

Take control of her life. Go after what she wanted.

She'd done that instinctively. She'd wanted a great career she could enjoy, so she'd gotten her degrees, applied at colleges, interviewed, and landed the job at St. Louis Metroland Community College.

But what did she want now?

Zan Sinclair.

Her hand tightened on the phone. No. Sometimes you went after what you wanted. Sometimes you looked for the serenity to accept what you couldn't have.

Then cried to your best friend.

But her sister was on the phone, waiting for her pearls of wisdom—or at least her little pieces of grit that could someday become pearls. "Hon, you don't have to do it alone. There are all sorts of seminars and classes you can take that'll help you plan your career and set and reach your goals. Or better yet, find a friend to give you encouragement. Someone you can talk to when you're frustrated or scared, who can help you sort through your options."

"Someone to steer me in the right direction?"

"Or even suggest new directions when you're stonewalled." Vicky spoke with more excitement as the idea crystalized. Ronnie lived in LA. She knew all sorts of society people who could introduce her to great actors. "Pick a person who has experience in the career you're trying to break into. Get yourself a mentor."

"A mentor? Of course!" The quaver of tears had given way to a lilt of interest. "I know exactly the man I need."

"Man?" Vicky's heart sank.

"Of course. Alex is perfect."

He was. Vicky slowly leaned forward until her forehead rested on her students' papers. She wished she could hide between their pages.

Rather than sweep house for a clean romantic beginning, she'd just helped Ronnie find a new reason to hang on to Zan.

* * *

All during the red-eye flight to St. Louis, Zan had chewed on *worlds apart*, considering how he was going to approach Vicky, weighing all angles until his brain was bleeding. He'd finally decided on an incredibly brilliant first step—prove he could indeed fit in to her world. Ingenious.

Or so it'd seemed at the time.

Now, as he stood outside the Metroland Community College lecture hall, the ingenious idea seemed like so much self-deception, as real as reality television or beef that whinnied.

Still, he didn't have any other ideas. So he pushed open the door to her classroom, prepared to prove he fit in to her world.

He found himself in a tiny horseshoe of a room with four ascending tiers to his right, maybe fifty seats max. Only half those seats were filled.

He paused with his hand on the door. He was somewhat taken aback at how small and empty the hall felt, used to his several-thousand-seat amphitheaters stuffed to the rafters. Maybe he'd left his roots behind, after all.

No, they were still part of him. *This* was still part of him. He could do this. He released the door and slid inside.

Vicky was writing on the whiteboard in the front of the room. He was momentarily mesmerized by the sway of her hips in her slacks as she powered information onto the board. Her hair was down, and it shook like waves of brown silk as she wrote. It struck him anew how lovely she was, how beautiful her form, how creamy her skin.

In his periphery, the young woman nearest the door twitched her gaze to him then back to the board. Then her eyes jerked back to him, wide as dinner plates.

He took his admiring gaze off Vicky long enough to meet the student's curious look. She was a young woman with dark, almond eyes, curly black hair, and an intelligent look about her.

Confirmed when he put a cautionary finger to his lips and she immediately nodded. He relaxed slightly.

Then she poked the student next to her, who did almost exactly the same double-take, seeing him.

He suppressed a sigh.

In mere seconds, the rest of the class noticed him. The near-silence of the classroom burred with excited whispers.

At the board, Vicky put a finishing touch on her point and studied it. Then she blinked and straightened. A quizzical smile curved her lips as she turned. "What's all the buzzing about...?"

She saw him.

CHAPTER ELEVEN

Zan tried a tentative smile. Vicky blinked several more times at him, as if she couldn't believe what she was seeing. Her chest began to heave in a way that drew his gaze to her perfect breasts. When the tip of her pink tongue darted out and touched her lips, lust flooded him, so fiery and potent he wanted to plaster her against the whiteboard and kiss her right then and there in front of all those students.

Okay, that wasn't part of his plan to fit in to her world.

He walled off the lust, cleared his throat, and pasted on a non-threatening smile. "Hello, Dr. Brooks."

She shook her head and did not speak. Her blue eyes were dark with some deep emotion.

"Aren't you Alexander Sinclair?" blurted the curly-haired student who had first seen him. "The media star?"

"He's more than a star, Lana," another said. "Dr. Sinclair is one of the smartest communications scientists out there."

"Hey," a boy at the back of the class said. "We're a communications class. You want to teach us?"

"Junior college communications class." Vicky had finally found her voice, although her tone was deeper than he remembered, and throaty. "Level 100. Dr. Sinclair is far above all that."

He liked her husky, intimate tone. He could imagine that voice caressing him in a darkened bedroom where he'd tumble her into a large, soft bed...damn. He was supposed to be fitting in.

He thought ferocious fitting-in thoughts.

Until he saw the blush that rode her cheeks. She was embarrassed. Either she'd seen the lust on his face before he'd walled it off, or something else was bothering her. He frowned as he analyzed the bits that had just passed...oh. Level 100, junior college. Whereas he had graduate students at two separate UC campuses. Worlds apart, damn it. Now he understood.

He immediately set out to put her at her ease. Prove that he fit in. "Not at all, Dr. Brooks. It was in an intimate class like this where I got my start in communications. Don't let me interrupt, please. I'll just sit over here, out of the way."

He crossed the room to an open row of seats on the far side. He felt the students' eyes follow him. A soft whistle as he passed made him self-conscious.

Worse, it showed Vicky might be right. Sure, he'd come from this world, but he'd changed since then. People reacted differently to him now. He'd been so keen on seeing Vicky and proving that he fit in to her world that he'd forgotten he wasn't the same boy who'd come out of it—no matter how he felt on the inside. Inside, he was still a gawky boy, but outside, other people considered him attractive; they reacted positively and with admiration.

It was the first time that he wished they didn't.

He made it to the other side of the room and sat. Or tried to. The seat was small and didn't fit. Like nothing else could, it brought home exactly how much he'd changed. Then, he'd been a skinny fifteen-year-old. He'd grown a bit since.

Still, he managed to get into the seat, although not comfortably. He certainly didn't risk pulling up the mini tray that served as a desk.

Instead he laced his hands, set them firmly on his crossed knee, and aimed a sunny smile at Vicky.

She stared at him with a mixture of longing, frustration, and regret, all overlaid with a small ironic-looking smile. He didn't have to wonder what thoughts were going through her head to cause that complex look.

They were the same as his own.

She blinked as if she was waking up. Realizing she had a class to teach. The longing disappeared, replaced by brisk competence.

He silently applauded her. Oh, she was good. No one would know what a jumble of feelings was going on inside her. No one but him, because he could see the tip of the iceberg in her slightly jerky writing, the occasional spearing of her fingers through her hair.

No one but him, because he was feeling the same confused, hot feelings. Feelings he'd tried to submerge, tried to deny, but had finally given up fighting. Instead, he gladly embraced them. And her, if she let him.

He shifted in his chair. It really was too small. Not just small but hard. What did they make these things out of, granite? With little flecks of Legos for added comfort. Probably to keep students from nodding off during lectures.

Vicky turned from the board at that moment. Her stare hardened on him as he squirmed in his chair. Glancing around the classroom, he saw why. *All* other eyes were on him, and the young woman nearest him was starting to drool a little.

He stilled abruptly. Folding his hands on his lap, he gave Vicky a small smile.

Obviously, if he was going to fit in to her world, he would have to try harder.

* * *

Vicky stared at Zan Sinclair in consternation. There he was, sitting like a lion in the middle of her herd of gazelles.

Why now? She had finally accepted she'd never fit in to Zan's world. It had brought an inner serenity.

Yet here Zan was, trying to fit in to hers. And failing, but he looked so cute squirming in that tiny chair, trying.

Maybe...just maybe she could meet him halfway.

"Okay, that's it for today. Read chapter seven for next week..." Vicky trailed off. Nobody was listening to her. The instant she'd said "that's it," the whole class had jumped up as if choreographed and rushed to mob Zan.

"Sign my notebook, Dr. Sinclair?" Rusty, a soccer player taking the class for core credit was first to slap his spiral notebook onto the seat's arm next to Zan.

"Sign my textbook? To Lana." Lana thrust her big *Communications* hardcover under his nose.

"Sign these?" Cheerleader Trixie pulled down her already low-necked sweater to expose plenty of cleavage and offered Zan a black indelible marker with a grin.

Vicky shook her head and suppressed a smile.

Zan's lips twitched. "I'll sign notebooks and books. Did everyone hear Dr. Brooks announce the reading?"

There was a general embarrassed sort of murmur as Zan extracted a slim pen from his inner suit coat pocket and slashed his signature on Rusty's notebook then looked at Lana expectantly.

"She said chapter seven." Lana grinned triumphantly.

"Correct. To Lana, for remembering chapter seven." Zan signed her book.

While Zan was signing, Vicky watched, marveling how he took time over each student, asking things like "What is your favorite part of this class?" and "What's the best thing you've learned from Dr. Brooks?"—despite his looks and money, he was a teacher through and through, there was no doubt. To her surprise, her students actually gave him intelligent, thoughtful answers; like a parent, she'd been afraid they hadn't been listening at all. Nobody left after the books were signed, but they all peppered him with questions, which he answered patiently and good-naturedly.

"Lana." Dr. Thoms W. Rekerton, chair of Vicky's department, swept in. "Where in the blue blazes have you been? I've been waiting for your report...*hello*, who's this?"

"Dr. Alexander Sinclair," Lana said brightly. "He's been talking with us, Dr. Rekerton. Isn't that *wonderful?*"

"What?" Rekerton's face looked like a squished lemon. "You've been chit-chatting here all this time, while I've been waiting for you?"

Even if Vicky hadn't heard the rumors, that sour face and jealous whine would have told her the story. Rekerton, head of the English-Communications-Journalism department, was also Lana's "adviser." Everybody knew he really used her intelligence and ambition to further his own mediocre career, taking credit for her writing.

His nickname was "Rocketman," for the speed with which he jumped to take credit for everything not nailed down.

Plus, Vicky suspected, he slept with Lana. She hoped for Lana's sake that nickname didn't also reflect his performance in the bedroom.

"But...but Dr. Rekerton," Lana said. "It's Dr. Alexander Sinclair. He's a *star.*"

"A star?" Rekerton jerked as if struck.

"Yes," Lana said. "*Revealing Secrets*? And Dr. Sinclair teaches communications to the stars."

"Oh, *that* Sinclair." Rekerton had made no secret of his desire to join the Big League. He must have realized here was his opportunity.

He scuttled up to Zan, his smile bright enough to take out a few city blocks. "Dr. Sinclair, how wonderful to meet you in person. Say, I haven't received your reply to my offer to coauthor a book with you."

Zan briefly closed his eyes; when they opened again, they were cool. "I'm sorry, I haven't seen it. When did you send it?"

Rekerton huffed. "I emailed it over two months ago."

"It must have gotten misfiled. My apologies, Dr...?"

"Rekerton." He grabbed Zan's hand and worked it like an oil rig. "Thoms W. Rekerton, the W stands for William. I'm department head. Go on, ask me."

"Ask you." Zan's gaze narrowed in a way that made Vicky understand he knew he wasn't going to like this. "Ask you what?"

"Ask me to read someone." Rekerton was still pumping Zan's hand despite Zan's increasingly strained smile. "I'm a whiz at nonverbal communications."

"I'm sure you are." Zan finally just pulled his hand from Rekerton's. Surreptitiously he gave Vicky a tiny roll of eyes. "You don't have to prove it to me."

"Of course I do! That's what the book is about, isn't it? I'm calling it *William's Nonverbal Tells*. Get it? William Tell, William's Tells?"

"Your middle name, yes. Clever. But I thought you wanted me to coauthor the book."

"Oh sure. We'll tack on *and Alexander's Calls*."

"Ah." Zan thumbed the bridge of his nose. "Why don't you email me again. Hopefully it won't end up misfiled this time."

"Great!" Rekerton pointed suddenly at Rusty. "He's thinking about soccer. And his girlfriend."

Rusty cleared his throat. "Actually, I was thinking about the party tonight—"

"Partying with his girlfriend." Rekerton beamed.

"Um," Zan said.

"She," Rekerton pointed at Trixie in her cheerleader's uniform, "is thinking about the game."

"No, I'm not—"

"And *you*, Dr. Sinclair. She's thinking about you."

Vicky rolled her eyes. As if he could miss the young woman's heated gaze on Zan.

Trixie gasped, "He's right! I was thinking about Dr. Sinclair. I was wondering if he's between girlfriends."

Rekerton pumped air. "See? I'm a comm whiz. She's thinking about you too." He pointed—at Lana.

Lana's face flamed.

"Thank you," Zan said. "But that's enough."

"How else can I prove I'm worthy of sharing a book with you, Dr. Sinclair?" Rekerton grinned. "See how flushed she is? How she's licking her lips?"

"Really, *enough*." Zan leaped to his feet, palms held up like twin stop signs. Vicky, too, had seen where this was going.

But Rekerton ground relentlessly on. "She wants to have sex with you. Here. Now."

The silence was profound. Lana was blushing so hard Vicky was surprised she didn't spontaneously combust. She went to the young woman and put a comforting arm around her.

"Shall I give you more?" Rekerton said eagerly.

"No!" Zan backed away from Rekerton. "No. I have to..." He pointed toward the exit. "I have to use the restroom."

"I'll come with you," Rekerton said.

"Absolutely not." Zan held up his hand like a traffic cop. "I'll only be a minute." He was already at the door. Vicky knew he was leaving to stop

Rekerton's hurtful spewing. "Be right back." He disappeared out the door so fast he left a jet trail.

"Show's over, everyone," Vicky said. "Get to your next classes. I want to talk to Dr. Rekerton alone."

The rest of the students cleared out almost as quickly as Sinclair. Lana, after one pain-filled look at Rekerton, ran out, hands covering her face, tears dripping from behind her palms.

The instant the door shut on her last student, Vicky spun to confront Rekerton. "That was inexcusable."

Rekerton's gaze was on the door. As if he hadn't heard her, he said, "Sinclair's quite a man, isn't he?"

"Yes." Vicky flushed as the thought of Zan's kiss intruded. "But that doesn't excuse your comments about Lana—"

"And I bet he's hung like a horse."

That silenced her.

Rekerton leaned close. "Do you think he'd like to sleep with Lana?"

"Wh-what?"

"Sinclair. Since he wasn't impressed with my communication prowess. Maybe he'd feel more kindly toward me if I let him sleep with Lana."

"*Let* him?" Slimy confirmation, if she'd wanted it, that the sludge was taking advantage of his student. "You think you own her? That she needs your permission to sleep with him?"

Rekerton reared back, surprise on his face. "She wouldn't."

"*He* wouldn't. Alexander Sinclair would never do something like sleep with a student he was *supposed* to be guiding and nurturing. *He's* got too much integrity."

Rekerton frowned. "Are you implying something?"

Not implying. Saying very clearly to a supposed communications whiz. "What do you think you accomplished with that display?"

"Now Sinclair knows how good I am."

"He certainly can see exactly what kind of man you are—at the cost of hurting Lana deeply."

"Lana?" Rekerton snickered. "I didn't hurt her. She's a young randy student who gives it away."

"You *idiot*." Vicky flung a furious hand toward the door where Lana had disappeared only moments ago. "Can't you see she has feelings for you? It's bad enough you run her ragged between your research projects and getting your dry cleaning, but to abuse her like that in front of everyone is inexcusable."

"You have no right—"

"I have every right. And so does Lana. She has the right to get an education without harassment, and especially without your emotional manipulation—"

"Shut up." Rekerton's head turned toward the doorway.

Where Zan Sinclair leaned, obviously listening to every word.

"This isn't over, Brooks," Rekerton muttered. He swept out.

As he passed Zan, Zan knocked his shoulder, challenging-male style.

Then Zan sauntered to stand before her. "You really tore into him. I've never seen you so angry."

Vicky's cheeks felt almost as fiery as Lana's. "How much did you hear?"

"Rekerton is a dumbshit. I have integrity." Zan smiled. "I'm incredibly proud of you."

"Wh-what?"

"I was furious with him. I left before I punched his face. But when I came back to cut him a new one, you were already taking care of it. You stood up for Lana. Brilliant. You're not just a teacher who stuffs young minds with information. You see real people and help them grow in a healthy manner. That's why I'm proud of you."

She gaped at him. From the light in his eyes, he really was proud of her.

It meant he did fit in her world, at least in this one supportive way. The heat in her cheeks shifted, spread through her entire body.

Suddenly the lecture hall door swung open. The dean of the college himself trotted in, clapping thin hands. "Dr. Alexander Sinclair, my daughter Trixie just told me you'd graced us with your presence. What an honor, what an honor!"

The dean was a bony, jowly man, like an old hound dog on two legs with bottle-thick glasses. He was invariably upbeat, totally at odds with his mournful appearance.

Zan gave Vicky a *what can you do?* shrug and smile and turned to the dean. "Hello. And you are?"

"John McAllister." He snatched one of Zan's hands in both of his—Zan had very large hands compared to the dean—and shook. "Dean of this fine institution. Such an honor, Dr. Sinclair."

"Thank you."

"Would you like to lecture here while you visit?"

"Well, I'm only planning to be in town a few days."

"Excellent! You can use room 205 for your office while you're here."

"Hey," Vicky said. "That's my office."

"I don't need an office," Zan said. "I was just visiting this class—"

"Excellent!" McAllister said. "This class is yours."

"No, I—"

"In fact, you can have all Dr. Brooks's classes if you want them. She's not tenured. I'm sure she won't mind."

"*I* mind." Zan retracted his hand to fold arms over his chest. "Dean McAllister, I'm here specifically to visit Dr. Brooks." He glanced at Vicky. She read, *Now maybe he'll stop pushing you out of the way.*

"You're visiting Dr. Brooks?" McAllister blinked big brown eyes behind his thick-lensed glasses. "But why?" He scratched his chin as he looked between Vicky and Zan. "Visiting, hmm...Oh."

Zan gave Vicky another glance. *He's getting the idea.*

"Visiting." McAllister's cheeks went bright pink. "*Oh.*"

"Oh?" Vicky frowned. "Oh...oh, no!" She glared at Zan. *He got the idea, all right.* "Dr. Sinclair isn't visiting me for...well, not that. Not personally. It's *business.*"

Zan pressed a palm to his forehead. "Academic," he agreed from behind his hand.

"Academic?" the dean asked.

"Academic," Zan said firmly, uncovering his face.

"Oh," the dean said. "You're writing a paper together?"

"No," Vicky said.

"Yes," Zan said. His eyes flicked to Vicky. *Play along with me.*

Vicky glared back. *Because that worked so well last time.*

"Wonderful!" The dean was glowing now. "Such prestige for our college."

Vicky said, "But—"

"We're not ready to publish yet," Zan said smoothly. "Please don't publicize this prematurely."

"Of course!" The dean put a finger to his lips. "Mum's the word."

The dean chatted up Zan another five minutes before a phone call from his admin reminded him of an urgent appointment. Even then, it was another five minutes before Vicky and Zan were alone.

Zan said, "Well, that could have been worse—"

"He thinks we're doing a paper! You and me. An academic paper!"

"He does." Zan nodded. "So let's."

"Let's what?"

"Write a paper together."

"*What*? We can't!" Vicky grabbed his arms. Either his sleeves were padded or his biceps were exceptionally thick. She dropped her hands at the sudden spike of desire. "Look, you can't write a paper with me. I'm a junior college professor. Your worldwide colleagues will laugh you out of the Communications Hall of Fame."

"There's no such thing as the Communications Hall of Fame." His lips quirked.

"You know what I mean." She couldn't help the slight grump to her voice.

His smile broke free. "I do. That's one of the reasons I think we should try it. You say we belong to different worlds, but we're not so different." He cupped her face in both hands. "I want to do a paper together. I want to very much."

I want. She froze. His skin on her cheeks was so warm. His touch electric. Libido that she'd smashed flat for a whole week roared to life. "I'd like to do more than a paper together."

His pupils dilated. "Me, too."

Her lips were suddenly over-full. She licked them.

His eyes dropped precipitously to follow. He stared at her mouth. "I was going to invite you to dinner."

"Dinner." Her voice was alarmingly breathy. "I don't want to go out."

He clenched his lids with a groan. "Me, neither." His hands dropped to her upper arms and tightened.

She dared, "Why don't you come back to my apartment instead."

He grabbed her hand and hauled her out of there with gratifying speed.

CHAPTER TWELVE

Outside her apartment door, Vicky dug in her shoulder bag for her keys, blindly because Zan was kissing her. His hands were on her, too, caressing her ribs, working their way slowly, artfully under her top, making her squeak and drop the keys just as she found them.

He pressed her back against the door, his tongue delving into her mouth. She squirmed against his hard possession, caught between granite muscles and hardwood and loving it. She forgot about her keys to clasp her hands behind his neck and try to drink him in in return.

The outer building door slammed. With a gasp, she released him and automatically tried to spring back, slamming herself into the door. Her spine rang with shocks of pain.

"Shh, it's okay." Zan pulled her to him and rubbed her back until the pain retreated. "Just someone leaving the other way. They didn't see us."

"You were watching?" Her whisper disguised the husky timbre to her voice, mostly. "I wasn't paying attention to anything except..." *except his hot, clever hands.* "I wasn't paying attention."

He grinned and released her to scoop up her keys from the hall floor. "Of course I was paying attention. I know you're shy—getting caught in public displays of affection embarrass you—and I want you to be comfortable."

He'd noticed her shyness and didn't ridicule her for it or try to talk her out of it. He took it seriously.

It was the sweetest thing anyone had ever said or done for her. But a lifetime of being told Ronnie was the outgoing, *normal* one made her say, "I have a right to get embarrassed. Being introverted isn't wrong or an illness."

"I know. Introversion isn't the same as antisocial—and it's not actually the same thing as being shy, either." He stuck her key in her apartment door. "Vicky. I know you're perfectly normal."

"You really mean that, don't you?" She scanned his face as he opened the lock and let them in, using every bit of communication smarts she had. "You're not just saying it to try to, um, get some."

"I really mean that." He wasn't looking at her as they walked in, paying close attention to extracting the key, shutting the door, and locking it. "Although, in the interest of fairness and honesty, I have to admit—I'm trying to get some too." He turned and grinned at her.

Her middle sparkled at his white, twinkling smile. She wanted to lick that boyish handsomeness from his chin up his honed jaw to his ear.

Her whole body flamed at the thought. She'd never wanted to lick anything but ice cream before.

He tossed her keys on the kitchen counter immediately to his left. "Anyway, you're being social. With me." He looked around. Kitchen and living room were split by a long, low counter. The bedroom door was off the living room at the far end of the counter.

"I'm not sure being with only one other person counts as being social."

"It counts for me." With another grin, he took her purse and briefcase out of her hands and set them on the counter next to her keys.

Then he swept her into his arms and carried her into the bedroom.

She gave a startled laugh at flying into the air. He spun her lengthwise to stride through the doorway. Her pumps dropped off her feet, her arms went around his neck, and she let loose another peal of laughter, this time in joy.

He laid her gently, almost reverently on the bed. She was relieved to note she'd tidied the covers this morning.

And then he stretched out on the bed beside her and lowered his head and kissed her, warm and soft. His hand spread across her ribs and caressed up until it cupped her breast. She forgot all about tidiness and shyness and anything whatsoever, immersed in male heat and taste.

In *Zan's* heat and taste.

He palmed her nipple awake. His tongue tempted her lips to part. She yielded—only to get a taste of him and lose control. Whimpering, she kissed him back eagerly, her tongue darting into his mouth, her hands digging into his hair, so silky for such a strong man. She arched to press her breast wantonly into his palm.

He chuckled. "Here in the bedroom, you're not shy at all. I like that."

"Oh!" Her lungs were pumping like bellows and her voice came out breathless. "Well...normally I am. But you inspire me."

"Good. Let me inspire you some more." He slid his hand down her ribs to her waist, where he burrowed fingers under her top. Spreading his hand on her skin, he slid back up, up, gliding under her bra. This time when he cupped her breast, skin heated skin.

She sucked in a breath. The few men she'd had sex with hadn't bothered with her breasts beyond a grope or two. In fact, most had concentrated on getting her naked, and then once she was naked, on getting inside.

This simple touch, skin to skin, was frighteningly intimate.

He circled his mouth over hers, coaxing her back into a kiss. Within moments, the fear faded, and she accepted the feel of his hand on her breast as normal, then exciting, then electric.

Then he thumbed her nipple.

She reared up, jerking so hard she nearly ripped his hair out.

"Sorry," he whispered against her lips. "You're just so sweet. So responsive." He brushed her nipple again, more gently. "I've been thinking about this all week. Longer."

"Longer?"

"Mmm. I think I've been dreaming of this since I first saw you."

"At the conference?"

"No, before that. When you visited LA." He caught her nipple between thumb and forefinger and gently pinched.

"Oh!" Pleasure zinged through her. "Don't you want to...you know. Undress me?"

"We have all night for that," he said, and she shivered with intense delight.

Out in the kitchen, her phone rang, a muffled *Masterpiece Theater* theme.

"Do you have to get that?" Zan murmured against the skin of her neck. The heat of his breath sent trails of shivers down her body.

"Mmm?"

"That's your phone." His voice was rough as he nipped along the tendon of her neck. "Not the generic ringtone. Do you have to get it?"

Not the generic ringtone. The sense of his words filtered through. *Masterpiece Theater* was someone from the college. "Damn it," she muttered. "Yes, I have to get that."

As he rolled aside, she flung herself to her feet then stalked to the kitchen. Her phone deedled inside her purse, sitting on the counter where Zan had left it. She grabbed it, rummaged inside, and managed to get her hand on the phone just as it stopped ringing.

Phooey. It was four-thirty on Friday afternoon. Why couldn't it wait until Monday? She set the phone on the counter. "Missed it. They'll leave voice mail." She rather hoped they didn't.

She turned back to the bedroom and sauntered toward Zan, lifting her top and her bra as she came. His eyes darkened, and a bulge strained against his slacks. She stopped just outside the bedroom door to strip off both top and bra and spin them a couple times in her hand.

"Why don't you come here and do that?" he suggested silkily.

She smiled, slowly.

The phone rang again.

"Damn it!" There went being sexy. She threw top and bra just inside the door then stomped back to the phone. Punched answer. "*Hello.*"

"Dr. Brooks, it's Dean McAllister. I may have accidentally leaked your relationship with Dr. Sinclair."

"*What?*" Her nipples stood straight up.

"About you doing a paper together."

"Oh." Vicky stared down at her breasts. *False alarm, girls.* "Well, I suppose it's not the worst thing in the world if you revealed that to a few students."

"Um, not students."

"Or a few faculty members."

"Nor faculty. That's why I'm calling you first."

"First...? Dean McAllister. Who did you leak this information to?"

"A few newspapers."

"Define 'a few.'"

"Thirty or so. Maybe cable television news too."

Yikes. "Thanks for the warning." She punched End, wishing for a good old-fashioned landline she could slam.

She turned back to the bedroom to give Zan the bad news.

He'd taken off his shirt and tie and stood, bare-chested, next to her bed, dwarfing it with his strength.

Her jaw clunked, hitting the floor. It must have bounced back, though, because when she rubbed her chin, it was in place, if a little slack.

He held his arms out and considered himself. "You like?"

Thick muscles danced everywhere. "Oh yes." She sighed it.

He lifted his head and beamed a smile directly into her brain, obliterating deans and newspapers and cable. "Good. Come here."

She came. He folded her in his arms and kissed her. The heat shimmered between them, and she'd just managed to lose enough of her inhibitions to nibble her way down his neck to the muscles of glory when the phone rang again.

Not theme from *Masterpiece Theater.* No, this tune went rollin' rollin' rollin' on the river.

"Damn it!" She bonked her forehead against his chest.

"Hush." He stroked her hair. "You're trembling. You recognize the ringtone? Who is it?"

"Who else? My sister."

Zan's arms sprang open as if Ronnie had caught them here. With a grimace, Vicky stalked for the phone and snapped it open. "Hello?"

"I just saw a strange tweet."

"Define strange."

"I was trolling with a hashtag of #SinclairSecrets...to see if he'd tweeted anything to his producer."

"About acting?"

"Um...yes. But it brought up other things. Lolly Darling is throwing a fundraiser, and she expects Alex to be there."

"And that's the strange tweet?"

"No, Alex does fundraisers all the time. But then I saw he's writing a paper together with another communications professor. This is a very recent development, just today. And this person Alex is collaborating with—a *her*, mind you—teaches at a small community college."

Vicky stopped breathing.

"Of course I thought of you. But I know that's impossible."

"Impossible," Vicky echoed.

"Because you know how much it would hurt me if you got together with Alex, don't you?"

Vicky swallowed hard. "Even professionally?"

There was a guilt-wracking pause. "It could never be purely professional with Alex. He's too much man."

"Oh." Vicky's voice was mouse-small.

"And you know it would absolutely devastate me if Alex were *there*, with you in St. Louis, don't you?"

"Ronnie...I'd never... I'd never intentionally—"

"Good. I'm glad we understand each other." And then, as if none of the past week had happened, she sang, "Love you! Buh-bye."

"Bye." Slowly Vicky ended the call. She stood there a moment, shoulders bowed, remorse washing over her.

Zan wasn't romantically interested in her sister, but if Vicky had sex with him before his relationship with Ronnie was resolved, well. It would be very painful, and not just for Ronnie.

And why was Vicky even thinking "relationship"? Had anything suggested this would last beyond one encounter, much less three dates? Most of Zan's flings were over in weeks.

And Vicky...she wasn't like Ronnie and Zan. She wasn't hugely popular, couldn't laugh it off as *his loss*.

She'd be hurt the most.

"Come sit by me," Zan called from the bedroom.

She couldn't look at him. "Not yet."

"It's okay. I won't attack you."

There was something odd in his tone of voice. She turned to see his expression.

A small, self-mocking smile twisted his lips.

Her heart went out to him...until he patted the bed next to him and she was distracted by the muscles sliding under bronzed skin in his shoulders and chest. She clenched her eyes shut, but the image was burned on her lids. He was so damned sexy.

"It's okay," he said again. "I just want to talk."

"That'd be good." She sighed. "But you'll have to put your shirt back on."

"Ah." A pause. "Vicky, I understand the issue with your sister."

She peeked. He'd grabbed his shirt, so she returned to the bedroom, snagging her bra and top on the way.

He shrugged into the shirt but didn't button it. If anything, the framing made his chest muscles more lickably delicious.

She briefly closed her eyes. She was in so far over her head. When she opened her eyes again, her gaze was on the bed. "I don't know what I was thinking. I'd never hurt Ronnie like this."

"I understand," he repeated. "You think you've hurt your sister as she hurt you. That going further with me will hurt her even more. But it's not the same."

"Of course it's the same."

"You forget, I know Ronnie. And I'm coming to know you. Did you realize I was a small child?" Slowly, he started buttoning his shirt, as if his mind was elsewhere, and he didn't continue.

She paused fastening her bra. "You're not small now."

"Growth spurt. But it didn't happen until late in my teens. Almost too late." His hands fell to his lap and he added, hesitantly, "I was...bullied."

She sank down next to him. He was staring at his hands, now stilled. She took one in both of hers. "Tell me about it."

He burrowed his hand deeper into her clasp. She squeezed her encouragement. With a heavy breath, he began. "I was the only child of an intellectual mother. I spent most of my early life on campus with her, either reading or surrounded by adults. By the time I went to grade school, I was more used to speaking with grownups than kids my own age.

"So I used big words. I was ridiculed, spurned, but those words were the only ones I knew. Worse, I was shy. I didn't look other kids in the eye, and they thought I was stuck up. I didn't know that then. All I knew was that kids my age hated me. Bigger kids weren't shy about beating me up. And since I was small—most kids were bigger than me."

"I'm so sorry." She held his hand tighter.

He clasped hers in return, as if drawing strength from her. "I started studying martial arts. With my size then, it meant less learning how to defend myself than being able to distract the bullies with a few jabs before running away really fast."

She rubbed her thumb on the back of his hand in silent support. He gave her a tiny smile and continued.

"My life was hell until my first year of high school. We moved to a small bedroom community. I wanted to take some advanced classes my school didn't offer, so the principal sent me to the nearby junior college. A sympathetic adviser there enrolled me in Introduction to Communications. And it opened my eyes. The mystery of why kids hated me was suddenly clear. I started saying 'hi' to everyone, making eye contact, and the high school kids started liking me. It was the first thing I'd done in my life that worked. I drank in everything I could about communications. Around that time, I had my growth spurt and became strong and physically attractive. With the changes in my behavior and my looks, I became well-liked and then popular."

"And then very popular."

"Yes. But the point is, none of it ever would have happened if not for that adviser. Those junior college classes. So I'll always have a soft spot for small-town professors. And I *always* remember who I was. That scared, misunderstood kid. He's still inside me."

* * *

Zan gazed into Vicky's eyes, willing her to see his vulnerability, his sheer need for her. Her pupils dilated to black velvet pools. He fell into her beautiful eyes, forgetting her need for distance, forgetting everything but how sweet her lips had tasted.

A *bbbrrring* like an old-fashioned landline interrupted him.

Vicky blinked. "That's not mine."

Zan sighed and released her hands. "My cell." Still, he hesitated.

"Shouldn't you get it?" Vicky said. "It might be important."

"You're right." Zan pulled his smartphone from his pants and checked the readout with a glance. "It's Nate. May I?"

"Of course."

He hit connect and put the phone to his ear.

"You have to come back to Los Angeles," Nate said without preamble. "*Now.*"

CHAPTER THIRTEEN

Zan winced and pulled the phone back. Nate was nearly shouting. "Calm down. Whatever it is, we'll handle it. I'm putting you on speaker."

"Calm *down...?* You try getting slashed open to the bone then tossed into a pit of sharks and see how calm you are. Get your ass on the next plane and back me up here. If I'm going down, I'm not going down alone."

"Nate, what is so urgent—"

"It's Lolly Darling, damn her hide. She's throwing a benefit auction for the local children's hospital."

"That's a good cause. What's the problem?"

"The problem is what she's auctioning. Us."

"Us? You and me?"

"All the eligible bachelors she can sink her hooks into. If you ask me, it's really for her daughter, who needs to get laid."

"Nasty, Nate."

"But true. You've met Lolly Junior."

Zan's gaze meshed with Vicky's, and there was a wry tilt to her brows. She hadn't met Lolly Junior, but she had met Lolly Senior. "When is this shindig?"

"Saturday night."

"Next week?"

"No, you ass. Do you think I panic that easily? Why would I interrupt you after you took so much trouble to sneak out of town to visit your little teacher? *Tomorrow.*"

His little teacher. Zan gave Vicky an apologetic glance. She was gazing at him in horror, and who could blame her? "His little teacher" was hardly subtle...then the last word Nate said seeped through Zan's brain.

Tomorrow?

"What? Nate, I can't."

"There is no 'can't,' Zan. There is only 'my butt is on that plane.'"

"Just because you've decided to play nice for Lolly—"

"I didn't *decide* anything. Lolly called in a favor, and I *have* to go. And buddy, you owe me for helping you with Ronnie Rivers so you could play smoochie face with that pretty little brunette of yours, remember? If I have to go, *you* go. You owe me."

"Damn. Wait. I have an idea." Zan turned to Vicky. He'd apologize for Nate's colorful phrases later. "I need a date. I'll give you the money to bid on me—"

"Not me!" Vicky raised both hands. "You don't need a simple date, you need a glamorous one, which I proved at the Gala I'm definitely not. At a billionaire bachelor charity auction? My not fitting in will be even more painfully obvious."

He made an impatient noise. "I fit in your world, of course you can fit in mine. But it doesn't matter, because I need you!"

"No, you need *Ronnie.* She knows all the scripts. She can navigate the horde cave of the Lesser Dragon."

"Who?" Zan scowled.

She waved it away. "The point is you need someone to save you from Lolly and her daughter, right? That's Ronnie."

"No. She'll think I'm making a subtle play for her."

"Hey," Nate said from the phone. "I don't care who you get to bail you out, but I'm calling your PA and telling her to book you on the next flight home. So make your plans quick." The line went dead.

Zan looked her in the eyes. "Vicky—"

"Zan." She shook her head.

"I like hearing you say my name." He gave her a quick kiss then sighed. "Though I can hear the 'but' coming."

"Yes. *But* you know I'm right. There's no way I can glam up by tomorrow, not without Ronnie's help, and Ronnie still thinks of you as hers. There's only one course of action." She grabbed his phone from his hand and, after a pause where it looked like she was figuring the screen out, punched in a number. As it started to ring, she offered it to him.

He only gazed at her, pleading with his eyes.

"Hello?"

The phone was still on speaker. He clenched his jaw. He couldn't believe he was doing this. He took the phone. "Hello, Ronnie."

"Nice of you to call, Alex." Ronnie's sugary, icicled tone said it was anything but nice.

Vicky flinched.

Zan got angry. Enough with the coy, nasty games. "Don't you start with me, Ms. Rivers. I got my credit card bill."

There was a shocked pause. Then Ronnie said in her normal tone, "Oh, pooh. What do you want?"

"I need a date for Lolly Darling's bachelor auction."

"Well, you know I'd love to help you out. Naturally."

Lovely. A new game. "But?"

"But I have something that day."

"You don't even know what day it is."

"Doesn't matter. I'm busy every day." Her tone hardened. "You're seeing Vicky, aren't you? You're cheating on me with my sister."

His gaze cut to Vicky. She'd paled. His hand fisted. Damn her sister for subjecting her to that. "Yes, I'm seeing your sister. But *we are not cheating on you*. What's more, I think you know that."

"I know nothing of the sort."

He wished he could see through the phone and glare some sense into her. "Veronica Brooks, grow up. Your sister may not be a supermodel, but she's pretty and smart and nice and works hard. You could learn a lot from her if you'd just open yourself to the possibility that she might be light-years ahead of you in the things that really count."

"Don't care." Ronnie hung up.

* * *

Vicky stared at the phone, horrified with her twin. How could Ronnie let Zan down when he was so obviously in need?

Then Zan started in on her again, wanting *her* to be his date to the charity auction. She told him to call one of his other glam girlfriends. He said he didn't want anyone but her. He pressed her until she had to retreat into the broken record technique to hold him off.

When he realized he was badgering her, he paled and stopped talking altogether.

He was so upset and distracted, Vicky drove with him to the airport to make sure he didn't run into anything. She saw that he picked up the right ticket and got to the right terminal for his flight back to LA.

Naturally, the minute she left the airport, she started having second thoughts. Sure, she didn't fit in his world. But he'd been so desperate.

Was it possible an embarrassing, horribly out-of-place date was better than no date at all?

Of course not. Glam was his world. He'd be fine.

Vicky was hunkered down in her living room chair, stewing, when her phone rang with Ronnie's ringtone. She punched answer and didn't bother with saying hello. "Veronica Brooks. You should have gone with him!"

"Are you kidding? Even if I wasn't hurt and mortified by my own twin cuckolding me, there's no way I'd attend one of Lolly Darling's stag lineups for her daughter."

"That's for men."

"What?" Ronnie snapped.

"Cuckold. It's specifically a woman cheating on her husband."

An exasperated beat. "I don't care. You stole my boyfriend."

"He wasn't yours to steal."

Outraged silence.

"Ronnie, you know it, and I know it. You and he were over long ago. You're just not admitting it."

"I was going to win him back," Ronnie blurted. "You were supposed to be my wingman and help me get him back!"

"And it didn't work. Now Zan needs you. Time to get over it."

"No!"

"Then if I go to the auction in your place, will you glam me up?"

Ronnie said a rude word and ended the call.

Leaving Vicky to stew some more. Talk about an epic fail. She hadn't been a good wingman for her sister, and now Zan would pay the price. Ronnie would have fit beautifully in his world as his glamorous escort, but without her, he had nobody.

Nobody but Vicky.

Vicky clutched the phone hard. Seeing Zan look so lost and needy, knowing what he'd faced as a boy to get where he was today... It tugged at her heartstrings.

She pressed the phone to her chest. She suddenly realized the question wasn't how Ronnie could let Zan down when he was so obviously in need.

The question was how could Vicky let him down?

He had no one but her.

She jumped to her feet. She'd do it.

She could have used Ronnie's help. Without it...she'd just have to think like Ronnie. She got online and reserved a ticket for an early flight to Los Angeles then called Zan's phone and left a message that she would be his date.

Then Vicky girded her loins and went shopping.

* * *

Saturday night. Vicky should have been lounging in a hot tub of bubbles with a glass of wine and a good book.

Instead, she was choking on her hair.

For the third time that night.

She'd spent all Friday night shopping, her mantra of "what would Ronnie do" leading her to pick a sleek red cocktail dress with a long skirt, gold shoes made by Torquemada the Grand Inquisitor, and a long blonde wig. She'd dropped exhausted into bed after midnight. Three or four times, she'd startled awake from a sound sleep to remember an item, write it down on her bedside pad, and drift off again. So when the alarm had shocked her out of bed, she'd groggily dressed for work before remembering why she was getting up so early on a Saturday.

She'd thrown everything in a carry-on suitcase, stopped at a Target to buy the things she was missing, and, now extremely late, had driven her little car like a robbery getaway to the airport, barely in time to get through extensive security before boarding the plane.

Zan, picking her up at the airport, smiled and told her not to worry—he'd engaged a dresser and makeup artist for her. He'd thanked her profusely for agreeing to this then dropped her into the hands of Satan's little imps.

They'd plumped, creamed, and astringented her— or was that astringined?—until she knew what bread dough felt like. One of the hairdressers had taken the Rapunzel 5000 wig she'd bought and twisted, pinned, and teased it into a coiffure fit for a princess. It had taken three of the imps to squeeze her into the dress she'd bought at the Glam Gowns and Straitjackets Emporium. They'd painted her face with stuff used for street art then plopped the wig on her head and fastened it on with industrial rivets. Okay, hairpins, but they felt like rivets.

Hours later she was ready, just in time. Zan picked her up in a different car, a sports coupe. He'd told her she looked beautiful, shoveled her into the coupe, and took off. She thought *she* was a fast driver. He drove like the Stig on a *Top Gear* racetrack.

The coupe's top was down. Gale-force winds blew the wig into disarray within a mile, although the wig itself stayed on her head, thanks to the rivets. The wind pulled part of the hairdo down. As Zan took a corner at three Gs, hair flew into her mouth, and an ill-timed inhalation took it straight into her lungs, choking her the first time.

She grabbed the tress and managed to pull it out of her windpipe. Because she wanted to look like Ronnie—maybe even make some of the society people think she *was* Ronnie—the blonde wig hair had something called "body," which meant it originally had belonged to a racehorse. It certainly galloped off every chance it got.

At Lady LaLa's mansion, Vicky got out of the car by grabbing the door and heaving herself out. She kept hold of the door, trying to balance on her tall toothpick heels. She was just congratulating herself for her uneventful-if-not-graceful exit when Zan shut her door—while she was still holding on to it. She stumbled, and a curl of her wig hair got trapped. She managed to right herself but tore the hank of hair. Eh, at least she was free of the door. Naturally, she promptly got another tress tangled in the sequined strap of her tiny shoulder bag.

Stray hairs kept stealing into her mouth and nose, trying to asphyxiate her. The last straw was when the hair snagged in an older gentleman's dentures—she didn't even want to think how that had happened.

It wasn't the only part of her glam disguise trying to kill her.

Her heels were tall and wobbly and tried to send her plummeting down every staircase they could find. The skirt was full-length, 1950s fashion style, tight to the knees and then flowing like a flower to the floor. Every time she took a step, it wrapped around her ankles like plastic wrap and helped the shoes trying to pitch her to the ground to be gored under the deadly sharp stilettos of the women or steamrollered by the pounding heels of the nervous stallions...er, bachelors. The strapless bodice of the dress was the opposite of her sister's gaping lemon dress, so tight and low-cut that her breasts kept bubbling out. She'd caught her nipples peeking twice already. The lady who sold her the dress had pushed some chunky jewelry on her last-minute. The necklace beat her collarbones with every step until her skin was bruised, and the matching dangling earrings, while pretty, dragged her earlobes down to her shoulders.

Whiny. But the fact was, she was not very comfortable here, and her clothes weren't helping.

On the bright side, she was still better off than all the studs...er, men.

A dozen filthy-rich bachelors milled in the reception area of Lolly Darling's mansion. The women eyed them up like haunches of prime beef.

Some did more than eye. As Zan dodged "accidental" gropes, he clung to Vicky's arm as if she was a Titanic life raft and his name was Leonardo DiCaprio. She could have told him not to bother. Look how well that had turned out.

Lolly greeted them as they came through the door. "Darling!" She presented her cheek to Zan, who dutifully pecked the air beside it.

Then it was Vicky's turn. Lolly bent to her cheek.

"You *dare* show up here," the Lesser Dragon hissed in her ear, "after what you did to me at the convention? Bitch."

Vicky reared back in surprise. All this hate, because she'd stopped the woman from hurting a well-intentioned student? But before she could reply, Lolly fastened on to both arms and cried, "Darling! So good of you to come."

"Um...thanks?"

"You're so welcome! Enjoy!" Lolly released her with a prick of her nails and turned to greet the next guests.

Wow. Ronnie was right. Lolly sure held a grudge.

As Zan led Vicky in, she darted a glance over her shoulder. "This is starting well."

He smiled. "Sarcastic much?"

She smiled back. The moment sang between them.

Broken as, like iron filings to a magnet, women with hungry eyes surrounded him.

"This is worse than I thought," Zan groaned as he extracted them from the mob. "Stay with me?"

"What if I have to use the restroom?"

"Hold it."

"I'll do what I can."

For the next hour, Zan gripped her arm so hard she wondered why she hadn't lost circulation. Plus side, no matter how many times she tripped, she never went down. The man was a rock of support.

But at dinner, he had to release her—though not to eat. Lolly had seated her daughter—whose name Vicky never discovered so she thought of her as Lolly Junior or the Lesser Dragonette—on Zan's other side.

Lolly Junior kept trying to go fishing for Zan's wedding tackle. He swatted her away like a mosquito.

Vicky bore it all with equanimity, knowing she was here for one purpose, to save Zan from getting gobbled up by the Lesser Dragon and her Lesser Dragonette daughter.

Until dessert.

Lolly rose and tinkled a little bell. "Ladies. We will now leave the gentlemen here so they can get ready for the auction while we enjoy dessert. Come." Her bosom jutting like a ship's prow, she led the women out of the room.

Vicky half-rose but hesitated. She didn't want to leave Zan. She especially didn't want to leave Zan to join the other women sailing out like luxury cruise liners, putt-putting along with her own tug-boat soul and jet-ski heels. She glanced at Zan, who shook his head. Relief filling her, she sank back into her seat.

Then Lolly Junior rose, revealing a gown cut to her navel and slit to the same, so fashionable the Emperor with the New Clothes would have found it baring. It was in danger of falling off if she breathed wrong.

Zan, perhaps sensing what was coming, snared Vicky's upper arm.

Sure enough, as the Lesser Dragonette sashayed past Vicky, she grabbed her other arm. "Upsy daisy, little chicky." Adding a hand on Vicky's elbow, she yanked.

Zan held firm. Vicky felt stretched like a tug-of-war rope.

Nate Winters, on Vicky's other side, leaned past her. "Let her go, Sinclair. Let's just get this over.

Why are you so worried? You have your angel to buy you."

"Me, an angel?" Lolly Junior tittered. "Why, Nate Winters, how charming you are. Maybe I'll buy you instead of Sinclair."

Nate went gray.

"Or I'll buy you *too*. I'll have you both!"

Nate and Zan exchanged a horrified look.

Lolly, in the doorway, clapped her hands twice. "*Now*, ladies."

"Let's get going, Little Miss Lambkin," Lolly Junior said.

Vicky assumed all the farm references were meant to imply she was a hick, but they missed the mark, pain-wise.

Until the other woman dragged Vicky to her feet by nearly pulling her arm out of its socket. That was physically painful, made worse when Lolly Junior brayed, "I can't wait to introduce you to all my upper-crust friends. You can tell them about your van down by the river!"

"That's *enough*." Zan's tone was low and vicious as he shot to his feet and grabbed the Lesser Dragonette. "Let her go." He peeled the woman's fingers away from Vicky's arm. "I don't care what the fallout is. Vicky, we're leaving."

Vicky was almost free when the Lesser Dragonette started shrieking. "Ow, ow, ow. Zan, you're hurting me!"

"What's going on?" Leda Loper called from the doorway. The Greater Dragon.

"Nothing," all four of them called.

"Good." The Greater Dragon gave them a stern look. "I will stay to make sure the bachelors get ready. The rest of you, please assemble in the dessert room. *Now*."

"Zan, I'll go." Vicky touched his arm to gain his attention, almost blown away when she saw the depth of caring for her in his gaze. "We'll get through this."

"Are you sure?"

She thought about saying "absolutely" for all of a second. As closely as he was reading her now, he of all people would know she was lying. "Not totally. But sure enough to give it a try."

He searched her eyes a moment more then gave her a tipped smile. "You're a brave soul. All right. But only if you let me know the moment you're done with their nonsense."

"I will." That she could promise whole-heartedly.

When Zan released the Lesser Dragonette, she must've taken it as giving in because she simpered, "You boys go get pretty now. The little lamb and I are going to get better acquainted." As Zan growled, she dragged Vicky off.

At the doorway, Vicky cast one look back at Zan. He pointed toward the front of the house and raised an inquiring brow. He'd really leave if she wanted, despite Nate and the Dragons, despite the consequences. Her heart warmed.

She gave a little shrug and smile in return. Communicated with her eyes that she could handle this. She'd be in full view of half the company. How bad could it be?

CHAPTER FOURTEEN

The Lesser Dragonette pulled Vicky into a huge room filled with low light, high shine, and rich *everything*. There, to Vicky's utter surprise, Lolly Junior released her.

"Let's see how you do without your rich protector." She bared teeth in a malicious grin.

Vicky scanned the palatial room. Tables dressed better than she was groaned under dozens of serving plates, each stacked with desserts less like food and more like art forms in sugar and spice. The masterpiece was a cake city sprawled across one entire table, bigger than any she'd ever seen, with tiers and bridges and whole continents in sugar. In the middle soared a skyscraper of a dozen or so frosted layers. Next to the Burj Khalifa of cakes was a table loaded with pies, pre-sliced and ready to be scooped onto wafer-thin china.

Lolly Junior shoved past Vicky to head for the long bar where a bartender set out rows and rows of exotic drinks from mojitos to caipirinhas to platinum passions. Women flocked to the bar, plucking up drinks to sip.

Vicky took a couple cautious steps. On the back wall was a stage plus runway, rented for this event—at least she thought the platform was rented, although what truly trendy household would be without one?—but it didn't come close to dominating the room. Good grief, there was even a fountain burbling in one corner, flowing into a pond teeming with orange and gold koi. In the other corner chirped a cage full of birds from bright blue to yellow to red.

Since the walking thing was going fine, Vicky tried a normal step forward—and tripped. Heels, polished floor? She was a stilt walker on ice. She barely caught herself with a series of stutter-steps.

Someone tittered. She looked up. All around her, eyes held a degrading mix of derision and pity. For the first time in her life, she wished she couldn't understand nonverbal communication so well.

"*Look* at you." The Lesser Dragonette was laughing her head off. "Trying so hard to fit in. Not working, dearie. Don't bother mimicking your betters."

Damn it. This woman brought a whole new level to the meaning of class conscious. Vicky was already uncomfortable enough, but what really hit hard was how this would rebound on Zan. These were his people, this was his crowd. Many now stared at her with disgust. Nearby whispers expressed pity for Zan.

She'd failed him.

Vicky's shoulders slumped, and her eyes prickled. She clenched them. She had *tried,* so hard, despite her fears, despite her discomfort, to fit into Zan's world, like her twin. She'd failed Zan. What was wrong with her...?

With *her?* Her eyes sprang open, seeing the judgmental glowers. What was wrong with *them?*

"*Betters?*" She rolled her eyes at Lolly Junior. "Who are you, Maggie Smith in *Downton Abby?*" She kicked off her wobbly heels and spun away in disdain.

As she turned, the Lesser Dragonette stepped on the trailing hem of her dress—and elbowed her.

Vicky stumbled. The bottom of her dress stayed nailed under the Lesser Dragonette's size twelve. Vicky's nipples winked out briefly; then the bottom of the dress tore with a loud *rip* and her bodice snapped back in place, giving her a nasty case of nipple rash.

One arm across her smarting breasts, Vicky spun to nail the Lesser Dragonette with a practiced glare that had freshmen quivering in their shoes. The Lesser Dragonette's expression changed from gloating to dawning fear as she fell back a step. Vicky whipped her torn hem out of stomping distance, turned, scooped up her shoes, tucked them under her arm, and limped away, body straight in wounded dignity. She ignored the whispers around her. The ragged bit of dress dragged behind.

She thought about gathering Zan and leaving, but she'd be damned to let these full-of-themselves hoity-toits make her turn tail and run. Instead she headed straight for the drink table.

She'd just gotten her fingers on the stem of a glass of simple Chablis when someone grabbed her arm.

"Oh, no, you don't." Lolly Senior's fingers clamped into Vicky's flesh like a crab's pincer, her expression just as crabby. "Those drinks aren't for the likes of you—hey!"

Lolly's jostling Vicky's arm shook the Chablis. Some of it jumped out of the glass and splashed onto Lolly's dress.

"How dare you!" Lolly trembled with rage.

Vicky glared back twice as fiery. She'd had it with these so-called mavens of "polite" society—now there was some irony. "Maybe you shouldn't have grabbed me?" she suggested frostily.

"You're an ill-bred menace. And now that you're without your man to protect you, I'm going to do something about it."

And more irony—she was here as *Zan's* protection. She rolled her eyes. "What are you going to do, rude me to death?"

"Why you...you..." The Lesser Dragon snatched up a pie—lemon meringue from the looks of it—and waved it threateningly at Vicky. "This is for that insult you dealt me at CommuniCon, for ruining my dress, and for thinking you're so great!" She cocked her arm back.

Vicky's eyes widened. "That escalated quickly."

Lolly threw the pie; Vicky ducked. The pie sailed over her head.

Straight at a tall, thin woman with curly white hair, wearing a diamond as big as a duck egg between her breasts.

The woman had just enough time to gape before the pie hit her in the face.

A hush descended on the room, broken only by the burble of the fountain and the chitter of birds.

The pie plate peeled off, hitting the floor with a gong-like clang. A pancake of meringue was left behind on the woman's face, surrounded by curly white hair.

Vicky waited, crouched in horrified fascination.

The white mass slid slowly down the woman's face, falling with a plop into her cleavage. Only the top of the diamond showed like a floating egg.

Slowly, the woman wiped the rest out of her eyes. Her...red...eyes.

Vicky followed the laser-thin fire shooting from the woman's eyes. Her target was Lolly. She hoped Lolly understood the danger in that *you-are-road-pâté* stare.

But Lolly stomped her foot. "See what you made me do!"

Vicky only smiled, set down her glass, and backed slowly out of the danger zone. The woman stalked to the pie table, and as Vicky retreated, she heard the whisper of metal sliding across cloth.

"Hey! Where do you think you're going?" Lolly snarled. Vicky turned to run but Lolly marched around her, cutting off her escape. The Lesser Dragon had just grabbed her to harangue her some more when Vicky, from the corner of her eye, saw the duck-egg-diamond woman spin from the table, a chocolate cream pie in her hand.

She whipped it at Lolly.

Vicky bobbed out of the line of fire.

The Lesser Dragon, fixated on Vicky—had to admire the gal's focus—didn't even flinch. The pie hit her full in the face.

This time, even the birds ceased chirping.

The pan slid off, leaving a thick slab of goop, like a mud facial gone horribly, horribly wrong.

Lolly howled. "Steena!"

A large, angular maid, expression horrified, came trotting up. "Ma'am?"

"Take this...this person and throw her out." Her trembling finger pointed at Vicky.

Just before the maid turned to see her, Vicky slid to her right, away from the accusing digit.

She was only trying to give herself time to think. But it left Lolly's finger pointing at a bowling ball of an older woman in an unfortunate dress of red polka dots that looked like an outbreak of measles, who was busy sampling the cake.

Before Vicky could intervene, the Lesser Dragon spun and stomped off. The maid stalked up to Bowling Ball. "Madam will come with me."

Vicky said, "No, wait—"

"I beg your pardon?" The measles-garbed woman drew herself straight, a slash of frosting marring her rosy cheek.

"The mistress has asked you to leave." The maid grabbed the woman's beefy arm.

The *mistress*? Vicky wondered if being a style maven meant adhering to the bad old 60s—the 1860s. She tried again. "Lolly didn't mean her—"

"I will *not*." The older woman stiffened. She shook off the maid's hand. "I paid good money to get into this shindig, and I have my eye on the stud with the Tom Selleck mustache. I'm gonna take me a ride. Yee-ha."

Vicky clenched her eyes, but the image had already burned into her brain.

The maid grimaced. "Mrs. Darling said—"

"I don't care what Lady LaLa said. I'm not going!" The woman twisted around until the maid was between her and the cake.

"You are!" The maid grabbed the woman by the sleeve and belt and swung her toward the door.

"I'm not!" The woman counter-grabbed and swung the maid. The added momentum spun them a little too fast.

The maid tripped. The woman yanked up on her to keep her from falling.

The maid flew into the table.

She slid along it like a battering ram, shoving aside smaller cakes like a bus crashing through cars—then plowed directly into the Tower of Cake. Face first.

The impact shuddered up through the layers. Tiers wavered. The top collapsed onto the layer below it. Both layers slammed into the third. One by one, the layers toppled until the whole thing came tumbling down with a deafening *splat*.

Another silence. Even the fish seemed to stare in awe.

The maid scrabbled off the table, collapsing in a heap of arms and legs on the floor. She tried to blink, finally having to sweep hollows into the chocolate sponge.

"Anyone else?" The round woman, head tucked like a prizefighter, glared from side to side. "Anyone else want to try to take me?"

Vicky tensed. From the woman's white nostrils and pumping chest, adrenaline had short-circuited all but her fight-or-flight instincts, keyed almost exclusively to *fight*. If anyone touched a match to this powder keg...

The maid leaped to her feet, swept a mass of cake and frosting off the table, and flung it straight into the woman's face.

With a snarl, the woman ran at the maid and grabbed her in a truly magnificent headlock. Dragging the maid to the table, she snagged a pie and pushed it into her face.

As if it was a trigger, suddenly richly gowned ladies were grabbing pies and gobs of cake and throwing. Vicky ducked and covered as loud splats and smacks and shrieks erupted around her. It was worse than a pillow fight, edging into bikini mud wrestling.

Then she saw Lolly Junior steaming through the flung food toward her like an avenging angel—or, considering her petulant expression, an enraged toddler.

"How dare you! You've ruined everything." She launched herself at Vicky.

The Lesser Dragonette's weight shoved Vicky stumbling into the table of pies. Shrieking, Lolly Junior tore at Vicky's dress, her jewelry, her hair— the wig came off. Thanks to the riveted hairpins, half her scalp came with it. Vicky yowled and pushed the Lesser Dragonette off—unintentionally launching her face-first onto a row of coconut creams.

The table broke. Lolly Junior landed on her belly on the floor. Pies skidded down the table halves to pelt her. The backless gown was no protection.

The Lesser Dragonette wailed. Vicky dropped her shoes and sprang to her aid, picking off pie plates and throwing them away so fast she accidentally Frisbee-d one into the birdcage. It hit metal with a ker-*whang* and clattered to the floor, leaving bent and broken mesh. Birds came to investigate and began to hop out. One by one, they launched into the air.

"Get me up!"

Vicky grasped the Lesser Dragonette's wrist and pulled.

The Lesser Dragonette came to her feet. Her gown didn't come along. As she staggered up, her dress, weighted down with pie, came off her shoulders and slid wetly down her body.

She was naked underneath.

Vicky groaned but was already moving. She scooped up the only available cover, three pie plates, and plastered them strategically to the Lesser Dragonette's body.

A sudden *whirr* of feathers in Vicky's ear startled her. She leaped to one side.

Birds flew around the room, calling and shrieking. A trio pecked at the lumpy mess on the table that had been the cake tower. Another two were practically washing in blackberry pie.

"*What is going on here?*" Leda Loper's shriek cut through the catfights.

Vicky spun toward the doorway. Around her, women froze in poses that would have looked more appropriate on a bunch of snowball-fighting kindergarteners on a school playground. Slowly, they also turned.

The Greater and Lesser Dragons stood in the doorway. Behind them, tall and forbidding, were the dozen bachelors.

The famous billionaire bachelors the women had come to impress.

One of the bedraggled messes whimpered. Another sighed. The bowling ball muttered, "Guess I can kiss that ride with Mr. Mustache goodbye."

Zan broke out from behind Leda Loper.

Vicky sighed. Now Zan would see how spectacularly she didn't belong in his world. The almost-night in her apartment would have to do.

She blinked suddenly scratchy eyes and grabbed herself to try to hold it together. Her fingers squished in a thin a layer of lemon pie filling.

But Zan jogged toward Vicky arms extended as if he meant to sweep her into an embrace.

She held up her palms to forestall him. "I'm a mess."

"I don't care." He grabbed her and hugged her to him, hard. "Oh, damn, I've never been so shocked...so scared...so tickled in all my life." His abs where twitching as if he was either laughing or having a nervous breakdown.

Her reply came out in a wail. "But I've spoiled everything! The party, the auction...and I was supposed to *grace* your arm." She hiccupped. "It's a fiasco. I've spoiled your standing in society with this."

"Sweetheart, you'd never spoil anything for me." Zan leaned back and smiled into her face. "Besides, you may have actually enhanced my standing. This set judges, not on propriety, but on boredom relief." He looked around at the women, some of whom were still fighting, some of whom were affecting *act-natural* poses trying to pretend nothing had happened, some of whom were stuffing their faces with cake, fighting birds to snatch the best pieces. "This certainly isn't boring."

Leda Loper appeared next to them, looking down her thin, aristocratic nose. "Sinclair. Your date's behavior is quite unseemly."

"See?" Vicky willed Zan to push her away.

But he only hugged her harder. "I do see, finally. I see that if I have to choose between my position in society and you, I choose you."

"Excuse me," Leda said.

"Zan, you can't!" Vicky said. "It'll affect your career."

"Not the important parts."

"*Doctor* Sinclair," Leda said. "You haven't lost your position in society yet. This girl, while impertinent, is...*interesting*. To say the least."

"*Girl*?" Vicky raised her head from Zan's encircling arms.

Leda pointed an imperious finger at her. "Young lady. When you've reached my age, you can presume to tell me how to speak. But for now, I'll tell you what's what."

"I'm not—"

"You have one chance to redeem yourselves. Both of you. You will attend a dinner party with me and my husband. And you will be on your best behavior."

Vicky shook her head. "But I have to get back—"

"If you want Zan Sinclair to be able to hold up his head in this town ever again, you'll rethink that, missy. And be at Le Hautaine tomorrow night at eight sharp."

* * *

Vicky slid into Zan's car, her head spinning. What had happened back there? He took off, but she barely noticed, even when the wind whipped through her hair. Her wig was long gone, and at least her own hair didn't try to kill her.

"Here we are." He stopped the car.

She blinked and came out of her thoughts. They were in a paved circular driveway, a fountain in its center. A swank, multilevel building was visible to her right. "The Hilton Hilltop?" Small for a hotel, though. There couldn't have been more than a dozen rooms.

"This is my home."

"I can't..." Her cheeks heated. But she sucked up her courage and faced him. "You can't want me to stay here."

"On the contrary." His gaze was direct and hot. "This is exactly where I want you."

"Oh." Her insides shimmered with the possibilities.

"Your carryon is already inside. Let me give you the grand tour."

He led her through a kitchen of gleaming appliances and cast-iron cookware, a living room of soft furniture in inviting colors, and a hardcore gamer's den.

The house was lovely, but not the stately mansion she would expect billionaire Dr. Alexander Sinclair to have. The rooms were good-sized, but she was surprised that it wasn't bigger. And the yard was anything but sprawling. When she looked off the back terrace, she saw another three homes on various levels of the bluff below.

Her face must've shown what she was thinking because he said, "Between the ocean and the mountains, there's not that much real estate around here. This way." He opened a door and set her suitcase inside. "Your bedroom. You can freshen up, and then we'll have a nightcap and talk."

"'Freshen up'? How strangely you society people speak. You mean clean up, right?" She nodded down at her torn, dirty dress; bits of dried pie and frosting had flaked off the whole way here like a sugary snowstorm. She didn't even want to think about her face.

"Whatever you need to do to be comfortable." He smiled. "Just do me a favor? Don't put on any makeup."

"Why?"

"Because I don't expect to see you in any when we wake up."

She blushed hot. "Oh. Okay."

CHAPTER FIFTEEN

Vicky got out of the shower, feeling a lot better about everything.

Then her phone rang, Ronnie's ringtone. Vicky's spirits plummeted again. She almost didn't answer. She wasn't sure if, after everything that had happened, she could take another of her sister's tirades.

"Darn it, I'm an introvert, not a coward." Besides, Ronnie was her sister. She answered her phone.

"I want to apologize," Ronnie said.

An instant's stunned surprise left Vicky momentarily speechless. She managed, "Who are you and what have you done with my twin?"

"Ha. Yesterday, after talking to Alex on the phone, I realized something. I'd been going after Alex so hard because getting guys has always been easy for me, and he's a challenge."

He sure is.

"Acting is a challenge too. I've ended up where I am because I've taken the easy road. Guys, modeling...in a way I'm jealous of you."

"Me?" That one took Vicky's legs out from under her. She collapsed onto the bed, comforter sliding against the skin of her thighs like silk—

She realized she was naked and sprang to her feet. "*You're* the supermodel."

"This isn't about worldly success. It's about character. You've got it." Ronnie paused. "Things don't fall into your lap, but you always seem to know how to go after what you want—and then you work hard and get it."

"Okay, now I know the pod aliens got you." Vicky padded to her suitcase for a change of clothes, stirring a light lavender scent from the soft carpet beneath her feet. "But what's that got to do with your acting career?"

"Everything has come so easily, I didn't know how to do something hard. Until what Alex said seeped through—about seeing your good points and learning from them."

"My good points." Vicky stopped pacing, amazed. "You're learning from *me?*"

"Yes. You have guts and determination. Smarts. Experience. I realized I should listen to your advice and follow it. So I set myself a small goal—taking an acting class—and within an hour I'd found one and signed up."

"Ronnie, that's great! Good for you."

"Thanks. But here's the cool thing. My first class was this morning and the teacher happens to be Flynn Roberts, Alex's executive producer. Guess what he said at the first break? He was gratified to see me taking my acting seriously. That I was working to better my craft."

"That's awesome."

"Completely. There's more. After class was over, I asked Flynn to coffee, to find out why I didn't get the role. He told me I was obviously just another pretty face while the character was slated to grow. He was afraid I couldn't grow with it. But after seeing me work hard in class, he changed his mind. I've got another chance at the role!"

"Ronnie, how wonderful! Congratulations." But even as Vicky said it, she realized now Ronnie wasn't just the pretty one; she was on her way to becoming the smart one too. Zan's match.

Vicky's heart froze. Years of boys and men picking Ronnie over Vicky rose. In a way, this was worse than her sister haranguing her. Now, if Zan and Ronnie got together, Vicky would have to be understanding and stand aside.

She'd have to pretend to be happy. After all, they'd be happy, two of the people she loved most in the world... *two*?

Oh, God. She loved Zan.

And if I truly love him and he wants Ronnie, I have to be happy for him. For them.

Damn it, I hate being noble.

Vicky collapsed on the bed again, no longer caring about sitting naked on the comforter. She crunched stinging eyes. "Good for you. But if that's all—"

"It isn't. Vicky, this isn't easy for me, but...I apologize. I didn't want Alex—I wanted what he could give me. I was being selfish. I officially hand him over to you."

Vicky's eyes opened slowly. Had she just heard...? "You're giving him to me." She shook her head. It seemed incredible. "Doesn't Zan get a say in this?"

"The guy?" Ronnie laughed. "Not if you're doing it right. So if you need my help glamming up, let me know."

"Thanks. Let me think about it." Vicky hung up.

How amazing. She loved Zan Sinclair. Even more amazing, they now had their chance at their clean start.

Her body thrilled at the idea.

But first she had to make it through Leda's intimate dinner. She chilled. While Ronnie had another chance at acting and Vicky had another chance to fit in Zan's world, when Vicky thought back to tonight's disaster, she shrank from the idea of glamming up for it. She glanced at the ruined dress, crusted with food. Yeah, that hadn't gone so well.

Her sister said she had guts and determination. Smarts. Experience.

Well, her smarts and experience told her she needed a whole new approach.

* * *

Dressed in jeans, casual shoes with socks, and a deep green sweater that she'd brought for flying home, Vicky followed the sound of soft music to the living room. Zan waited for her on the plush sofa. The music, some kind of lanky jazz, soothed her ears. Aromatic candles bathed the room in a glow of promise.

He stood when he saw her, glasses of wine in his hands.

He handed her one. "I didn't think you'd gotten anything to drink at Lolly's."

"Thanks. I was too nervous to eat or drink much." She accepted the glass and sipped. "Perfect," she sighed.

"I want to give you something else perfect." He sat and patted the seat next to him.

She immediately stiffened. Yesterday, at her apartment...things had gone so fast that she hadn't had time to doubt. But now, knowing what he intended, she was horribly self-conscious.

He quirked a smile, set down his glass of wine, and picked up a bottle of lotion. "Foot rub?"

"Oh, yes, *please*." She immediately sat down on the couch and swung both feet into his lap.

It startled a laugh out of him. "Only if you're sure."

"With those high heels? My feet are killing me. I've needed this all night. Since the Gala, actually. Before."

He removed one shoe and sock, pumped a generous amount of lotion, warmed it between his hands with brisk rubbing, then slicked it on her foot.

"Ohhhh," she moaned. "I think I'm in love."

"Forget chocolate and roses, forget kissing. Apparently foot rubs are the ultimate seduction."

"Hey, you try walking on your toes for hours at a stretch, and we'll see how receptive you are to a little foot seduction."

He worked the lotion into the ball of her foot, and she groaned again. He kneaded each toe, the heel, and used his knuckles on the outer ridge of her foot like a wooden ball massager. Each wrung a little moan from her.

"Switch." He reached for her other foot.

She kicked off her own shoe and pulled off the sock so fast it smoked, then stuck her naked foot in his face, toes wiggling.

He laughed. "So cooperative. I wish I'd known this about you when I was first trying to meet you or when I was begging you to come with me to Lolly's charity auction."

"What? And give you another weapon of mass seduction? You already have an unfair advantage with women, Sinclair."

"I don't want an advantage with *women*, Dr. Brooks. I want an advantage with *one* woman—you. Did I hear you talking with your sister before? Dare I hope that she's coming around?"

"Maybe. She got another chance at that role she's been slavering for. It put her in a good mood. We'll see if it lasts."

"Mmm. Sit up and I'll rub your shoulders."

"Oh, I definitely love you." She sat right up.

"You're so easy, Brooks."

"Everyone has her buttons." She spun her hair into a knot and offered him her aching shoulders.

He dug his fingers into her muscles until she groaned. He began massaging, and she groaned in rhythm with his kneading.

"Speaking of buttons...what are we going to do about dinner with Leda?"

She stiffened. He dropped a kiss on the back of her neck. His warm breath both tickled and soothed. She shrugged. "My sister offered to glam me up. But I don't know. That didn't work so well."

"I was thinking...what if we just go as ourselves? Slacks and shirts and whiteboard marker smudges?"

"Heavens, I'd love that. But what about your career? It's tied to the rich and famous set."

"I'm just a teacher who happens to be on television." He kissed her neck again, a little longer, then kissed a path down it.

She shivered at the hot progression of his lips. "A simple billionaire teacher. Besides, they're your social contacts, and more, your show's patrons. Who will underwrite your show, if not for the rich?"

"Communications students?" He nipped lightly.

She shivered harder. "I don't think students will buy ads on network television any time soon." She turned. Lifted her chin in unspoken invitation.

"Crowdfunding?" He dropped a kiss on her throat. "Sweetheart, it doesn't matter." He nibbled where he'd kissed. "Don't get me wrong. I've had a good run, and I've enjoyed it." He kissed up her throat to her chin. "But if I have to give it up, so be it. Nothing lasts forever. Except this."

He took her lips.

His kiss was gentle, sliding along her skin, but when he opened his mouth, she could taste the fire of his desire for her. Sliding her fingers into his hair, she opened her mouth to his in return. His tongue slipped inside her, along with a soul-deep sigh.

"I love you, Victoria Brooks." He nipped her earlobe.

She shivered. "You can't. We barely know each other."

"I know you're caring and perceptive and genuine." He took her mouth in a deep, lingering kiss. "I think about you when I'm not with you. I see us building a life together, me caring for you and you caring for me. I see us growing old together." He lifted her sweater and bent to kiss her breasts until her body was tingling and her nipples were tight. "If you love me too, we'll work the rest out."

He peeled her down to skin, kissing and caressing each exposed inch until she was fiery with need, then lifted her and carried her into his bedroom. He laid her reverently on the spread, rummaged in a bedside table drawer for something that crinkled and rolled, climbed onto the bed, and covered her with his body. "Ready?" The love and desire in his eyes was as brilliant as the night stars.

"For longer than you know. I love you too." She lost herself in the heavens of his dark eyes. Lost all sense of shyness and became purely herself. She spread her thighs, not in abandonment, but with a sense of coming into her own.

"I feel so attuned with you." He began moving, and she groaned. "As if we've always known each other."

"You said you were like me before you became famous." Her skin prickled as perspiration dewed her. "As a boy."

"You make me remember the best part of me." He moved faster.

"You've grown beyond it. You're better now."

"I'm richer. But better?" He paused moving. "I squashed my feelings and dated self-absorbed women rather than take the risk of a real relationship. Until you." He started moving again, harder, pushing her up the peak of no return.

"Zan...I'm...I'm..."

"Yes, Vicky. I'm *feeling* now. And I'm committing...*now*. To you."

She fell from the peak, and he came with her.

After, he tucked her into his body. Snuggling there, she gained the courage to ask, "So tomorrow...? With the Greater Dragon? How should I play it?"

He murmured, "Be yourself."

"Just me?" No blonde wig or cutting-chic dress? "You don't want anything better?"

"Sweetheart, I don't want anything *less*."

* * *

Vicky wasn't completely comfortable going to a nice restaurant in jeans and yesterday's sweater, so the next morning they went shopping. She tried on everything from slacks to a gem-studded cocktail dress but found herself happiest with a simple sundress, topped by a white silk sweater. For jewelry, Zan bought her plain gold hoop earrings and a shell necklace. Her shoes were white rhinestone Sketchers. No more tripping over her own feet in skyscraper heels for her.

She felt comfortable and stable—if a little short—on Zan's arm as he led her into Le Hautaine.

At the sight of lacquered golden wood, gleaming crystal, and crimson silk, her hard-won composure fled. A spigot of acid cranked open in her belly.

Zan might have come from her world, but he'd moved on since then.

"Dr. Sinclair!" The maitre d' rushed up. Or rather, in a black suit every bit as expensive-looking as Zan's Gala tux, and much too formal to be a simple maitre d', the maître d'hôtel. He clasped Zan's arms and planted not one, not two, but three kisses on Zan's sculpted cheeks, which, by the third kiss, were slightly flushed.

"Hello, Pierre," Zan said. "This is my colleague and very good friend Dr. Victoria Brooks. Are the Drs. Loper here yet?"

Doctors, plural?

"*Oui*, Monsieur. This way."

The natty man led them through the main dining room. Vicky was nervous enough meeting the Greater Dragon again, but she nearly turned tail to run when she saw who else was in the main dining room.

Lolly Darling sat at an elegant table with her entire entourage, including Lolly Junior.

The Lesser Dragon saw Vicky with a double-take. Then she lifted her chin—and turned away.

A pointed snub. Vicky had laughed it off before, but now she was with Zan. She wished the floor were a drain and she was water.

Until Lolly Junior and the rest of the table followed suit, turning, noses in the air, in a slo-mo the whole room could see.

Snubbing, not only her, but *Zan.*

Vicky's spine snapped straight so fast the whole room heard the crack. Was this second grade? Was this the eighteenth century?

Hell, no. This was here and now, and both she and Zan were human beings deserving of respect. Her lioness roared to the surface. Sure, she was introverted, but this was more than enough for any one soul to have to take.

"Again with the cut direct," Vicky murmured. "Well, lady, here's the finger direct." She gave Lolly some special nonverbal communication as she breezed by.

A collective gasp at the table let her know she'd scored a hit.

They were escorted into a private dining room where the Greater Dragon (*Dr. Dragon?*) and her husband held court, and the true ordeal began.

After Vicky was introduced to Leda Loper's retired music-professor husband, Gerald, she started to sit.

Zan stopped her. He pulled out the chair for her and slid it under her as she hesitantly sat.

Leda Loper sniffed. "I hope she knows which fork to use."

Vicky's spine stiffened. She deliberately tried to relax. This was the high maven of Zan's set. She couldn't just give Leda the finger.

Zan seated himself next to Vicky and gave her hand a subtle supportive squeeze. When Leda began chatting about the Gala. Vicky kept her mouth shut.

"Please pass the pepper," Gerald murmured to her.

Vicky picked up the crystal grinder and set it in front of him.

"Both together, girl," Leda sniffed. "You pass both together, so diners don't have to hunt for one or the other. And never set them on the table. Pass hand to hand. Where did you find her, Zan? A barn?"

Vicky gritted her teeth and said, "Thank you. I'll try to remember that."

Later, Gerald said, "Pass me the breadbasket, Sinclair?" As Zan lifted the napkin-covered basket, Vicky said, "I'd like a roll, please."

"No, girl," Leda said, her tone plummy. "Never snatch one as they pass."

Stung, Vicky said, "I wasn't going to. I just thought Gerald could pass me the basket when he was done."

"Really, Zan, are you sure you know what you're doing?"

"I'm very sure, Leda." Zan's eyes were narrow and glittering. His hand clenched in his lap. His tense jaw shouted he was furious. One more crack and he'd deal with the Greater Dragon in no uncertain terms.

Vicky didn't want this to escalate. She could go home to St. Louis, but Zan lived here. She touched his hand and gave him a pleading look. His eyes stayed narrowed and his jaw worked a moment before he sat back, his hand relaxing.

She was very careful that, when she did get her roll, she cut a pat of butter using the proper knife and followed all the proper rules to eat. She was so worried about doing it right she didn't taste the roll.

Then her French onion soup came in a lovely handled crock. Actually forgetting her surroundings and nerves for a moment, looking forward to the tang of broth and onions, she dug her spoon into the thick melted cheese on top. The rich smell of beef filled her nostrils, and she closed her eyes and savored.

Until Leda *tsked.* "No, girl, always dip away from you! Honestly, Zan, teach the girl manners. It reflects badly on you."

"It reflects badly on *Zan*?" Vicky's eyes popped open. "You're penalizing *Zan* for *my* ignorance?" She set down her soupspoon, carefully, because she was trembling. Not with fear, but with rage, the inner lion filling her until she had to roar. "Dr. Loper. Pick on me all you want. I'm introverted. I haven't learned high society scripts. I may never fit in with the cream. And maybe I don't deserve being with Zan— but you know what? I'm okay with that. I'm okay with who I am." She slapped her hands on the table, leaned in, and glared directly into Leda's eyes. "But don't you dare pick on Zan for what you think is wrong with me. He's a brilliant teacher, kind and professional, and he's done more for communications than anyone in his generation. You *will* respect him!"

There was a moment of shocked silence. Leda Loper's cheeks turned bright red.

Then Gerald Loper started clapping. "Oh, *brava,* Vicky. Brava, my dear."

Leda's cheeks returned to normal. "Indeed. Well done, Vicky. I couldn't have said it better myself."

"Damn you, Leda." Zan's eyes were cutting narrow. "How dare you?"

"I had to make sure she wasn't a worthless twit like the rest of them, dear." Leda broke off a bit of her own roll and nonchalantly buttered it.

"What's going on?" Vicky looked at each set of eyes around the table; Zan's disgusted dark gaze, Gerald's twinkling green, and Leda's serene blue.

Zan tossed his napkin on the table. "Leda's my old communications professor. The one from the community college who rescued me when I was clueless."

"This was a test?"

"Absolutely." Leda nibbled her roll. "Zan doesn't need a woman who looks good on his arm. He needs one who understands him and can defend his inner child—a sweet child, by the way—so that he doesn't have to hide his emotions or distance himself from other people. You passed with flying colors."

"But...but I'm an introvert. How can I have passed?"

"You're caring and kind, and you stand up for others. Social scripts—eh, you can learn them." Leda smiled. "I did."

"Wait, what?"

"Where do you think Zan's 'set' came from, and how do you think I got to lead it? I was a small-town community college professor until Zan brought Gerald and me out here fifteen years ago. We didn't fit in either. I learned some of the scripts then made a place for myself. It took a few years, but—"

"You learned all the high society scripts in just a few years?"

"Of course not." Leda's lips curved. "I learned a enough to pass and made up the rest. You can do that too. Make your own place in the world, girl. Make your own place in life."

"I'm not a girl."

"No." Leda smiled fully. "You're not."

Zan stood. "If I'd known you were planning this, I'd never have agreed to come. We're leaving."

"Calm down, Zan," Leda said. "This was as much for her as for you."

Vicky's head hurt. *For me?*

Gerald said to Zan, "You run with a tough crowd, boy. We had to find out for sure if she's tough enough to last. Now you know. But more—*she* knows."

"She knows she's strong. She can stand up to the worst we can hand out." The Greater Dragon appeared almost smug.

Vicky put aside her own surprise to touch Zan's clenched hand. "These are your friends. It's okay. They only did this because they want what's best for you."

"If they want to be my friends, they'd better rethink that attitude." He spoke to Vicky but his black gaze remained burning on the Lopers. "They'd better want what's best for *you*."

Leda's smile faltered as her blue gaze twitched between Zan and Vicky. She touched fingers to her breastbone. "Zan...I'm so sorry. I didn't know...well, how could I? It's only been a week."

"It's been longer than that," he sliced at her.

"However long it's been, you love her," Leda said simply. "And you want what's best for her. That's what love is, isn't it? Wanting what's best for the other person?" She smiled at Gerald.

He gave her a gentle caress on the cheek then nodded at Zan. "You want what's best for her," he repeated. "But she wants what's best for you too. Let her show it. Stay."

Vicky slipped her fingers into Zan's clenching fist and tugged.

He stood stiffly for a moment longer then looked at her. "Are you sure you want to stay?"

"These are your friends," she repeated. "I'm sure."

* * *

At the next CommuniCon, in St. Louis a year later, Dr. Victoria Brooks paced the greenroom, about to present her paper in the main ballroom.

Nerves eating her, she paused pacing to glance out at a packed crowd. She started hyperventilating. "I don't know if I can do this."

She was speaking to her coauthor and husband of six months, Dr. Alexander Sinclair.

Zan gathered her in his arms. "Hush, sweetheart. You won't be alone out there."

She laughed, somewhat muffled by his strong, suit-coated arms. "Aren't you going to tell me to imagine them all naked or something?"

"No. You're an introvert. Your strength is your imagination—which means imagining them naked will only start your brain freewheeling."

"I love how well you know me." She looked up at him, his strong profile and his brilliant dark eyes that, right now, were warm with love.

"Remember that when we argue over the next paper we write."

"We weren't arguing. Discussing loudly, maybe."

"Loudly enough that the studio's nightshift security ran in with his stun gun drawn."

"True." She hugged him then let him go with a little goose. "Hey, I know what I can do. Lana's out there. I can focus on her." The bright student had dumped Rekerton and, after making sure every single student knew about him, had come to study with Vicky in LA.

"Great idea," Zan said. "She always has a smile for her favorite teacher."

Just then Vicky's phone chimed. "Forgot to set it to vibrate." She took it out. "Oh, how nice. It's a text from Ronnie wishing me a broken leg."

He peered over her shoulder. "That's theater-speak for good luck. How is she?"

"In production with her new show and loving it. She says it's not going to win any awards, but in my opinion, it's already won one—Happiest Supporting Actress."

"Thanks to you."

"Thanks to her hard work. But we both helped." Vicky took a deep breath. "Okay, Ronnie succeeded at acting, and I took on the Dragons. Why am I afraid of a few people? With you at my side, I can take on any crowd." She started forward.

He grabbed her hand. "And with you at my side, I don't have to be any less than fully myself."

Hand in hand, to a round of applause, they went out to the podium together.

ABOUT THE AUTHOR

Mary Hughes (written Hug-he's but possibly pronounced throat warbler mangrove) writes smart and sassy stories of action and love.

She's a bona fide computer geek and performing flutist. (And piccolo, but we don't talk about that.) When this USA Today Bestselling Author isn't busy finding the missing </> tag or blowing her lungs out, she's on the couch reading or binging on The Flash, Elementary, NCIS, or Wynonna Earp...and petting the cats that inevitably end up on her lap.

Mary's online and would love to hear from you!
Newsletter
http://www.maryhughesbooks.com/Newsletter.html
Facebook
http://www.facebook.com/MaryHughesAuthor
Twitter http://www.twitter.com/MaryHughesBooks
Instagram
https://www.instagram.com/maryhughesbooks
BookBub
https://www.bookbub.com/authors/mary-hughes
Goodreads
http://www.goodreads.com/author/show/279140.
Mary_Hughes
Website http://www.maryhughesbooks.com/
    Blog http://maryhughesbooks.blogspot.com/

BLACK DIAMOND JINN
(A HOT SF/FANTASY NOVELLA)

Have sex, avert doom, save the world.

The Mayan Doom is real. Government witch Amaia Jones has the spreadsheet to prove it.

Amaia is a desk-bound research wizard, living uncomfortably in the shadow of her famous Venus-magic parents. Then she discovers the world is ending. Tonight. But her bulldog of a boss not only refuses to believe her, he won't give her the secret to calling the one force powerful enough to help—the jinn. Amaia turns to her mental guardian angel, Rafe, the darkly handsome presence who has comforted her since her parents died.

Rafe has a secret of his own. He's a black diamond jinn, one of the deadliest and most powerful of his kind. He's detected an enemy ruthlessly using blood sacrifice to stoke Y12 public panic. Rafe needs to get into the human realm to stop the Doom, but he can't unless Amaia calls him, and she is threatened by his scorching sensuality.

Amaia's guardian angel is a stunning jinni and suddenly her job is far more complicated. Jinn take their pound of flesh in exchange for magical help, but the only flesh Rafe wants is hers, taut with delight. Sounds great, except Venus magic is what drove a wedge between her parents. But her alternatives are rapidly dwindling, and with four hours to go on humanity's darkest night, the only alternative to surrendering her flesh may be surrendering her life.

This title contains explicit sexual language and may not be suitable for all readers.

Enjoy the following excerpt from Black Diamond Jinn:

I stared up, and up, at six and a half feet of hard male.

He stood before me, fists on hips. Loose pants barely covered him, riding low on those taut hips. Nothing at all covered his granite chest, a flawless bare canvas for the flame tattoo licking one pec.

"Oh my God. You're real."

He was the Rafe of my imagination, but sharper, leaner. Harder. Dreamy chest muscles jutted fiercely in reality; six-pack abs were hard boulders. His well-cut mouth and square jaw were honed to an almost cruel degree. His black hair, bound in a braid, cascaded over his chest, the tail teasing the dent of his navel.

Black diamond eyes gleamed with an inhuman intelligence, a brilliance that encompassed galaxies. In them blazed a will that could defy the stars and a power that could wipe out entire civilizations, and perhaps had.

Those eyes marked him as jinn.

I swallowed hard. My guardian angel was a powerful jinni—and stunning in more ways than one. Physically compelling, haloed in a beautiful, deadly magic, the reality of him raked me with feelings from joy to heart-pounding terror—and instant arousal.